Hawley Smart

The Master of Rathkelly

A Novel: Vol. II.

Hawley Smart

The Master of Rathkelly
A Novel: Vol. II.

ISBN/EAN: 9783337031527

Printed in Europe, USA, Canada, Australia, Japan

Cover: Foto ©Andreas Hilbeck / pixelio.de

More available books at **www.hansebooks.com**

THE MASTER OF RATHKELLY.

THE MASTER OF RATHKELLY

A Novel.

BY

HAWLEY SMART,

Author of

"BREEZIE LANGTON," "SOCIAL SINNERS," "HARD LINES," "FROM POST TO FINISH," "BAD TO BEAT," "CLEVERLY WON," &c. &c.

IN TWO VOLUMES.

VOL. II.

LONDON:
F. V. WHITE & Co.,
31, SOUTHAMPTON STREET, STRAND, W.C.
1888.

PRINTED BY
KELLY AND CO., GATE STREET, LINCOLN'S INN FIELDS
AND KINGSTON-ON-THAMES.

CONTENTS.

—◆—

THE MASTER OF RATHKELLY.

THE MASTER OF RATHKELLY

CHAPTER I.

"A NATIONALIST CONCLAVE."

MIKE CASSIDY, like a dog who has fought, lies in his cabin licking his wounds, and brooding over his wrongs. He has received notice to quit his farm; and his hatred of the Eyres has become so morbid that it almost amounts to a disease. Ryan and Terence Flynn, too, have awakened the fiercest animosity in his breast, not because he has fought with them—bad-tempered man though he was he had all the national respect for a free fight—but they had interfered with his scheme of vengeance. Then, too, he had been exposed to the jeers of some of Mr.

Casey's adherents, who had lost their money over the defeat of the Repealer. Unfortunately for himself, he possessed a bragging tongue, and a great weakness for whiskey, and after two or three glasses of punch, was much given to boasting of what he could do or would do, and so on.

Now he had given out very ostentatiously before the race, that whatever might win it would not be Rory, capping the assertion with a strong expletive, and the remark: "He'd moind that." Whatever he had intended doing, the result had only been a lively scrimmage, in which he and his friends had got decidedly the worst of it. Naturally given to speechifying, and taking considerably more interest in politics than in work, Mike Cassidy had for years been known as an orator of the shebeen house, or as we describe it in England, a "pothouse politician." The doctrines of the League exactly suited him, the idea of paying no rent found much

favour in his eyes; and if like the leaders of
the movement, he could attain the blessed
privilege of being comfortably paid for the
indulgence of his natural garrulity, he would
have considered himself to have attained a ter-
restrial paradise. He had gradually become
a well-known and trustworthy subordinate of
the chiefs of the conspiracy; he had been
personally made known to Messrs. Last and
Carmody; he was just such an instrument as
these terrorizers required. An unscrupulous,
discontented, bad tempered man was a tool
ready-made to their hands. The work that
McDermot had initiated must be continued.

"It is necessary, me bhoy, to cut the
combs of these landlords a bit; and the most
stiff necked ould tyrant amongst them in
these parts is Ratcliffe Eyre. Bedad, he
thinks he owns the people, as well as the
land."

"That's so," rejoined Mr. Last, "and their
wives an' daughters, too, because ye don't

happen to be one of themselves, they turn up
their noses at ye, as if ye were so much dirt
under their feet."

Mr. Last is still a little sore about his unfortunate debût at the Callowtown ball; so
it came to pass that these two illustrious
senators, when not impeding the business of
the nation by their interminable prolixity at
St. Stephen's, rushed across the Channel and
indulged in inflammatory harangues, flavoured
with as much sedition as they deemed prudent
to put into them, the result of their exertions
being that Callowtown and its neighbourhood were simmering with indignation against
all law and order, and regarded the landed
proprietors in their midst pretty much as
the "Sans Culottes" did the old French
nobility in '93.

Mike Cassidy registers a solemn vow to himself, that the Ryans and Terence Flynn shall
be made to pay dearly for interfering between
him and his projected vengeance on his land-

lord. He is still haunted by the idea, too, that Terence must know all about his attempt on Mr. Eyre's life. True, he has never heard anybody even whisper that Mr. Eyre has been shot at, and that of itself Mike Cassidy regards as a " quare thing." Naturally suspicious, and rendered doubly so by being aware that he has placed himself within the clutches of the law, Cassidy cannot help fancying that Mr. Eyre is only biding his time to throw him into prison on a capital charge. Again and again he wonders what he can have dropped on the road that night which Terence possessed himself of, and might lead to his identification. If he could think over it calmly, he would see that whatever he might have done there could be no evidence against him, and men in these days are not hung upon conjecture. Whatever Mr. Eyre or Terence might think, they neither of them had seen him at the time the shot was fired ; but, callous as some murderers are to fear or remorse for their crimes, this immunity is not given to all of them, and Cassidy felt it were good for him if both Mr. Eyre and Flynn were, what he euphoniously termed, " got rid of."

Cassidy was in this uncomfortable state of mind when he received a message from McDermot bidding him come up to his house, as there was a subject of national importance to be discussed. This man was a very prominent member of the League, and one in whom they placed considerable reliance ; a combative man, and who had warned the Harkhallow Hunt off his lands without prompting from anyone, but this had suggested to Messrs. Carmody and Last the striking of a tremendous blow at the landlords in a body, and their idea was nothing less than the boycotting of the Harkhallow Hunt.

" Landlordism must be stamped out," said Mr. Carmody. " Popular opinion would be against us if we put them under the soil they have stolen, but we'll do the next thing to it, we'll destroy all their amusements, and make their lives a burthen to them ; and what's more, we'll bring them pretty close to the workhouse to wind up with."

When Cassidy arrived at McDermot's, he found a little conclave assembled in that worthy's parlour, who were discussing this subject, with much animation and also much spirits and water, and it was speedily agreed amongst them that the mandates of their leaders should be carried out, and the Harkhallow Hunt boycotted without delay. Except as a political demonstration there could be nothing more uncalled-for ; it was the very end of the hunting season, it was doubtful whether the hounds would meet half-a-dozen times more, and therefore it would have been easy to give Mr. Eyre notice that permission to hunt over their lands would be withdrawn for the future, and this, signed by a majority of the farmers of the country, would necessitate

his giving up the hounds that his family had
hunted so long. But that would not at all
have suited Messrs. Carmody and Last. They
had confided to McDermot what they wanted
done, and that was that a regular mob should
turn out at one of the advertised meets, and
peremptorily forbid even the drawing of a
cover. They were exhorted to use both sticks
and stones should their mandamus not be
obeyed, and with all the casuistry of the old
story of " *don't* nail his ear to the pump,
bhoys," were urged to proceed to no violence,
though, as Mr. Last bombastically observed,
" If any of your bloated oppressors get hurt
in opposing the will of a down-trodden
people, their blood be upon their own head ! "

Nothing could have chimed in more
harmoniously with Mike Cassidy's feelings
than lending a hand in a little plot of this
description.

" He's a grate man intoirely, is that
Misther Carmody. It's a swate idea,

McDermot, and it's meself 'll be deloighted
to take a hand at the game. I only hope ould
Eyre will be out himself. And you too,
McDermot, ye've a little account with him
to square up, he has not paid for that clip on
the head he gave ye as yet. What's foive
pound for breaking in a fellow-craythur's
skull? A rock or two in one's pockets,
bhoys, will be moighty convanient that
mornin', our sticks, of course, unless anny
gintleman has a preference for a flail, which
is a swate weapon in a crowd, and moight be
handy amongst the dogs."

It was months since Mike Cassidy had
been so genial amongst his neighbours. As
McDermot said when reporting progress to
Mr. Last :

" Michael Cassidy is an invaluable recruit,
only anxious for *active employment*, and one
we can rely upon for annything."

Late events had thoroughly opened
Ratcliffe Eyre's eyes to the signs of the

times. A period of great agricultural
depression had swept over the United Kingdom, and landlords far and wide had been
compelled to grant a considerable abatement
of rent. There was downright distress
amongst the farmers, and they were no better
off in many parts of England than they were
in Ireland, but they bore it very differently
in the two countries. The English farmer
finding it impossible, even at reduced rent,
to get a living out of agriculture, gave up his
farm and started to earn his bread in some
other fashion. The Irish farmer, on the
contrary, clung to his land, and, even if he
could, was forbidden to pay rent by a
perfectly illegal organisation. Eyre recognised at once that professional agitators for
their own purposes had initiated a war of
classes, and that the strife between landlord
and tenant was likely to grow bitter until the
government mustered up courage to restore
law and order with a firm hand. He was

not the man to blench from the conflict; beaten he might be, but there was no doubt about it he would fight.

From the stand the fight at the brook had certainly been visible, but none of the spectators had in any way connected it with the race. That there had been what some of the gentlemen called, "a little difference of opinion," going on by the water was patent to all the on-lookers, but nobody troubled themselves much about such a trifling matter. The race was going on, and by the time that was finished the battle had about died out, still it was hardly to be supposed that the story of the fray would not reach the ears of the Rathkelly ladies before long. Norah ran down to the Castle the next day to congratulate her young mistress on her victory.

"Ah, we were all so plazed, Miss Katie, you can't think, to hear that Rory had won. We couldn't see from where we were, and I was so frightened at the fight besides. To think of the villains trying to prevent your horse from winning!"

"Why, what *do* you mean, Norah?" enquired Miss Eyre.

"I don't quite know how he heard it." replied the girl, " but Terence did hear some- how that Mike Cassidy had sworn that your horse shouldn't win, and he tould father, and shure enough when the Captain was bringing Rory down to the brook, Cassidy jumped out on the course and was going to baulk him, and father caught hold of him, and then they fought, an' then Terence went to help father, an some of the other bhoys went to help Cassidy, an' then it seemed as if everybody went to help one side or another, an' for a few minutes they bate each other dreadful. An' Terence got his head broke, an' father can't move his left arm this mornin'. But it's all right, the Captain got Rory in first, long life to him! an' you won, Miss Katie, you won!"

"Do you mean to tell us," said Mrs. Belton, "that Cassidy dared attempt to interfere with my sister's horse?"

"Yes, indeed," replied the girl; "an' father said afterwards that Miss Katie owed quite as much to Terence as she did to Captain Sturton."

"You're quite sure of all this, Norah?" said Mrs. Belton. "Your father, for instance, didn't catch hold of Cassidy because he *thought* he was going to interfere with the horse?"

"Ah! no, Ma'am—he an' Terence knew Cassidy was up to something, an' they just went an' stood by him to prevent whativer he was going to do. He's under notice to quit, ye see, Ma'am, and he swore no horse out of the masther's stables should win the race this year."

When Mr. Eyre heard the account of the fight by the brook from his daughters, a grim smile flickered round his mouth.

"I shall have to settle accounts with that scoundrel," he said, "before we part, and I've a presentiment he'll be paid in full."

"Shall you have him up before the magistrates?" enquired Mrs. Belton.

"I've nothing to have him up for, Gracie. Whatever he might have intended, thanks to Tim Ryan, he didn't carry it out. There's one thing I am delighted to hear, and that is that Mr. Casey and his friends dropped a good bit of money over the Repealer."

"But surely Cassidy ought to be punished, Papa?" said Katie.

"I've a tolerably long score to settle with him some of these days," rejoined her father. "Yes," he continued to himself, "it will be a case, before we've done, Mike Cassidy, of your life or mine, and you needn't think, if the chance is given me, that I shall stay my hand."

In consequence of Norah's story, Eyre walked up to Ryan's cabin, and had half-an-

hour's talk with the farmer and his wife.
Ryan corroborated his daughter's story in
every respect. Terence had told him just
before the race of what Cassidy had openly
declared, that "he would take care Miss
Eyre's horse didn't win," that seeing Cassidy
with two or three companions close by the
water jump, he and Terence had got near him
to prevent mischief, and that he had no doubt
as to what were Cassidy's intentions when he
sprang out of the crowd. As for the remainder of the story, Tim Ryan only laughed,
and added :

"Well, thin, yer honour, we just kept him
busy till the race was over."

Ratcliffe Eyre also wrote a note to Sturton,
telling what he had heard, and asking him
whether he considered there was any truth in
it. Sturton enclosed the two notes that he
had received, one of which Norah at once
identified as being in Terence's handwriting,
but the other was in an unknown hand.

Sturton further said that he had no doubt whatever of what Cassidy's intentions were, and that both Blake and Chester held similar views. He had also talked over the thing with Power, but the rider of Kate Kearney said he was too far behind at that part of the race to see what happened. " I am very glad," concluded Sturton, " that my unknown friend has been identified. If he interferes in politics to the extent you tell me he does, he is likely sooner or later to bring himself in contact with the troops, and if so, the opportunity may be given me of reciprocating his polite intentions."

Michael Cassidy's labours in the cause of the League had so far resulted in a broken head and the fierce enmity of two men not likely to spare him when their turn came.

CHAPTER II.

"A SISTERLY SKIRMISH."

Tom Chester was getting not a little dissatisfied with the way his affairs were going. He had been beaten in the steeplechase, but he did not so much mind that, Loadstone had run a good horse and quite justified his owner's good opinion of him. Then again, Miss Eyre had won, and that was all as it should be, but the young lady's conduct as regarded himself was very much the reverse. He was very much in love, and very much in earnest, but he could not conceal from himself that he was not making the progress in her good opinion that he could wish. She ordered him about in pretty imperious fashion, still there was no disguising the fact that, though it delighted her to play the tyrant, she showed

no signs of her heart being touched by his
devotion. Mrs. Belton, looking on at the
comedy with an amused smile, murmured to
herself: "The saucy chit, he stands too much
in awe of her. Ah, Mr. Chester, if I didn't
think it unwise to interfere, I could give you
a valuable hint or two, just now."

The true state of the case had never in the
least dawned upon Mrs. Belton. It never
occurred to her that her young sister could
have fallen in love with her own old admirer.
There was nothing at all singular in it to an
unprejudiced observer, but it never entered
Mrs. Belton's head that it could be so, otherwise such a quick-witted woman as herself
would have arrived at some inkling of the
truth. She thought it a pity that the girl
did not fancy Mr. Chester, he was an eligible
parti, and Mrs. Belton, whose eyes had
been gradually opened to the present state
of the country, saw that rents in Ireland
were becoming a very precarious source of

income to landowners. Katie might do a good deal worse than engage herself to a man in Chester's position, and then a smile played round Mrs. Belton's lips as she thought, " I'm sure I was willing to engage myself to a man without half his advantages, if he had only asked me, but then," she continued, with a queer little *moue*, " I was over head and ears in love with him and that *does* make a difference."

Mrs. Belton comes down to breakfast one morning looking so radiant that both her father and sister involuntarily look at her for an explanation of her glad tidings.

"It's delightful, father. George is on his way home, says that he shall be in London almost as soon as I get this. I shall just have time for a good gallop from Ballater Gorse next Thursday, and then I must run over to meet him."

" Why, I thought you did not expect him till late in the autumn ? " cried Katie.

" No. The regiment is ordered home
six months before its time, and that makes
all the difference. I've got my house for
six months, and even now I don't know where
we shall be quartered."

" Well, I shall be very sorry to lose
you, Gracie," said Mr. Eyre, " but I suppose
you and Belton will have to determine where
you're to live. You must run over and pay
us another visit."

" Of course, father," replied Mrs. Belton,
laughing. " You'll see me here the next
hunting-season, at all events. The first thing
George will have to do, will be to buy me a
horse that can hold its own with these
steeplechasers."

Ratcliffe Eyre made no reply to his
daughter's badinage. Already he had a dim
foreboding that the days were fast approaching which would witness the extinction of the
Harkhallow Hunt. Though he had no idea
how very close at hand they actually were, he

thought the extreme badness of the times might before long necessitate the practising of economy. And though the giving up of the hounds he regarded as a thing not to be resorted to except in the last extremity, yet he conceived it might even possibly come to that.

On the afternoon of the day that Mrs. Belton had announced her approaching departure, Sturton and Chester called at Rathkelly. The latter had been assiduous in his visits ever since he had first made the Eyres' acquaintance, and was cordially welcomed by all of them, even including Miss Eyre, who, if she did not care for him in the way he wished, was not at all insensible to the glory of parading the captive of her bow and spear. Sturton on the other hand, popular though he was with its inmates, rarely put in an appearance at Rathkelly Castle, but when he did the result was pretty sure to make Miss Eyre rather hard upon her admirer, and somewhat petulant with her sister. It was,

perhaps, a little exasperating for the girl.
Sturton persistently ignored the fact that she
had grown up. He treated her with the easy
condescension one might use to a child, and
devoted himself entirely to Mrs. Belton. To
a hot-tempered young lady like Miss Eyre
this was simply maddening, and those immediately about her, although they might be
ignorant of the cause, could not doubt that
she was much dissatisfied about something.

"And so you're really going, Mrs. Belton?"
exclaimed Sturton. "I saw in one of the
military papers that the regiment had got its
orders rather unexpectedly. I wondered
then whether it would make any difference in
your plans."

"Oh, yes!" she replied. "I must go to
London, if it's only to arrange where we are
to pitch our tent next. I am afraid you can't
enlighten me?"

"No," replied Sturton, "but I have no
doubt that the agents can. Call in at Cox's

when you reach town ; depend upon it they will know."

" Thanks, Captain Sturton. One last gallop from Ballater Gorse, on Thursday, and then I'm off. Come and see the last of me. I don't ride now-a-days like Katie. As for seeing the last of her, I suppose we shall all do that ten minutes after we find."

" You needn't be disagreeable, Gracie," replied Miss Eyre, " because I happened to have the best of you last time we met there. She is dreadfully jealous of my horsemanship, Mr. Chester."

" Well, you can ride, you know," rejoined Chester vaguely, with a dim idea that he was getting into stormy water.

" Yes," observed Sturton quietly, " Miss Eyre can ride, and when she is on Rory, is riding about the best horse in the Hunt. But what matters who is first, or who is not? Never fear, Mrs. Belton, but what you'll ride with an escort the last day that ' We find him in Ballater Gorse.' If you leave your escort behind, well we can't help it. I shall do my best not to be in that plight."

" No fear," replied Miss Eyre capriciously, " though I don't suppose you would make any attempt to keep alongside of me?"

" Ah! You're very difficult to catch, you see," rejoined Sturton laughing, and with a half-mocking bow.

Katie's mouth twitched, and it was with some difficulty that she suppressed the sharp retort that rose to her lips. Why did this man persist in treating her like a petulant school-girl? She had felt inclined to rejoin: " Yes, you would break your neck for Gracie's sake, but not canter up the avenue for mine." Still, hot-headed as she was, a general sense of the fitness of things made the words die away upon her lips.

" Mr. Chester," she exclaimed, " come and see my flowers."

It was the early days of April, and not

likely, unless the flowers took the form of
crocuses or violets, that there could be any
to see; and a faint smile played about Mrs.
Belton's lips, as she thought she com-
prehended her sister's rather too transparent
manœuvre.

"Well," she said to herself, "it's the grand
audacity of seventeen. Katie has walked her
young man off on the most bare faced pretext
that ever young woman invented."

Mr. Chester also took this view of the case,
but he was speedily destined to be unde-
ceived; the object of his admiration, when
she had got him into the garden, turned out
to be in anything but an amiable frame of
mind. She was arbitrary, contradictory, and
let him say what he would it never was right.
In short, by the time their twenty minutes'
stroll was over, Tom Chester had about come
to the conclusion that Miss Eyre was not for
him. He was as much in love as ever, but
he thought that the asking this imperious

maiden to marry him would be simply hopeless on his part.

"I don't think she cares for any other
fellow," he muttered to himself; "but,
hang it all! it's pretty clear she don't care
a straw about me. I'd better ride a waiting race than go in and be said 'no' to,
right off."

One must be a good deal older than Tom
Chester to adhere to these arbitrary rules.
When one's heart is deeply interested one's
head is apt to get a little confused, and the
finish of a man's first love affair, like the
finish of his first race, is likely to be characterised by much want of coolness and judgment.

"You think badly of the state of the
country, Captain Sturton?" said Mrs. Belton,
after Chester and her sister had left the
drawing-room.

"Yes," he replied, "I do. Norah Ryan's
story is perfectly true. I have no earthly

doubt that, but for the interposition of her father, there would have been an attempt made to upset me at the brook. Not aimed at me personally, of course, but simply because I was riding a horse belonging to an Eyre."

"You surely don't think my father in any danger?" said Mrs. Belton anxiously.

"No, but it's hard to say what may be the result of such inflammatory harangues as Messrs. Last and Carmody indulge in. The rents I'm afraid will give trouble," continued Sturton. "And now, if you'll allow me, I'll ring for our horses. I see Chester is coming back from his botanical walk," and he glanced mischievously at Mrs. Belton.

"It's not quite good-bye," replied Grace, ignoring his look. "I shall expect to see you both at Ballater Gorse on Thursday."

"Without doubt," said Chester, who by this time had re-entered the room, and then the two men made their adieux.

" Well, Katie," said Mrs. Belton, "I hope Mr. Chester was pleased with——"

" What ?" replied the girl sharply, as her sister hesitated.

"The flowers, my dear. They must have taken a good deal of finding. What did he say to you ?"

"What should he say to me?" returned Miss Eyre demurely. " Mr. Chester's conversation is never very brilliant, and I think perhaps to-day it was rather below the average."

" Nonsense, you know what I mean, Katie, anyone can see that the man is over head and ears in love with you. He only wants a little encouragement to ask you to be his wife."

"Ah! he don't want any encouragement," replied the girl quickly, " it's just all I can do to keep him from speaking now."

" And why don't you let him speak ? he's a

good-looking, gentlemanly young man; and you might do worse, if you fancy him."

"It's a terrible thing to be a younger sister," was Miss Eyre's irrelevant remark.

"Why so?" asked Mrs. Belton.

"Because the elder ones think they have a right to manage your love affairs for you."

"Nothing of the sort, you foolish girl. I don't want to interfere. I was only giving you a little bit of advice."

"That's just what people say when they mean to make themselves extra disagreeable," said Miss Eyre.

"It's the first word I've said to you on the subject, and we'll not revert to it; though what you can see to dislike in Mr. Chester I can't imagine."

"I didn't say I disliked him," rejoined Katie.

"Then you have no business to play shilly-shally with him. You can't keep a man on and off in this fashion."

"I really don't see, Grace, that it's any business of yours," rejoined Miss Eyre angrily. "Perhaps I don't know my own mind. I'm very young, as everyone is always reminding me. In another ten years or so, you'll perhaps admit that I am grown up."

"Do as you like, my dear. I have said my say," rejoined Mrs. Belton, rising. "There's nothing to be angry about."

"I'm not in the least angry," exclaimed Miss Eyre, whose flushed face hardly confirmed the assertion; "but whether I like or dislike Mr. Chester is a matter that concerns only him and me."

"Quite so," rejoined Mrs. Belton, as she left the room.

Katie, indeed, was very angry—angry with herself, because she had allowed her fancy to stray into a strong feeling for a man who apparently had no regard for her; angry, also, because she felt the justice of her sister's reproaches about her treatment of Chester, and very angry with Grace, because she possessed that power of attracting Sturton which seemed utterly denied to herself.

"Why will they persist that I am so young?" exclaimed Katie fiercely. "I shall be seventeen next month, and I've been mistress of Rathkelly for the last two years."

CHAPTER III.

"THE BOYCOTTING OF THE HUNT."

"By Jove! what a lovely morning," remarked Chester, as he and Sturton, enveloped in loose overcoats, spun merrily along in a dog-cart to meet their horses at Ballater Gorse.

"It is, Tom. I don't know whether it is quite our last day; but I'm afraid it's the last season of the Harkhallow Hunt."

"Good heavens! what do you mean?" said Chester. "Old Eyre may be a ricketty life; but I take it his son will carry on the hounds. Why, it's a family appanage. The Eyres have had the Harkhallow for fourscore years or more."

"Yes," replied Sturton slowly, as he took

his cigar from his lips; " but if half I hear
from Blake and others be true, all these men
will be stone broke before two years are
over their heads. What can they do? Their
tenants can pay, but the League won't let
them, under threat of boycotting—new-
fashioned name for excommunication, murder
or mutilation. Good lord! to think in the
days of the nineteenth century that any such
tyranny as this should be submitted to by the
people."

" Ah, come, it's not so bad as that," returned Chester. " Eyre don't look as if he
was hard up yet. And, bless your soul,
his claret and his daughter are things to
dream of."

" Fancy you dream about that last, Tom,
perhaps more than is good for you. You
can't mean, seriously, to think of that petulant
school-girl? "

" She has rather a quick temper. I like
'em like that," replied Chester, as he flicked

his horse a little spitefully, drawing a smile from his observant companion, who saw how that luckless animal was doing penance for Miss Eyre's iniquities. " As for school-girl, it's nonsense to call her that. Why, she's out. We met her at the Callowtown Ball."

" Crept out," rejoined Sturton, laughing. " It's a way those precocious little monkeys have, even when there is a determined mother to hold such impulses in check, much more when there isn't ; but, never mind Miss Eyre, her charms or her tantrums. There, my boy, is Ballater Gorse, and a goodly concourse of habits and red coats by the side of it ; but halloa ! " and as he spoke, Sturton raised himself in the trap, and, steadying himself by the rail, continued— " What the devil is the meaning of all that mob in the background ? "

" Awful crowd to see the last crack meet of the season," said Chester.

" No, no, Tom," replied Sturton, quickly.
" It's a good deal more than that; neither
you nor I ever saw so many foot-people
about at a meet of the Harkhallow. What's
the row up there, William?" he continued, as
the dog-cart pulled up at the gate of a field,
and a smart-looking English groom led their
horses up there.

" Don't know, sir," replied the man, as he
touched his hat to his master. " They do
say," and he lowered his voice in perfectly
awe-struck tones—" that they ain't going to
allow the hounds to draw the cover. Ireland
is a queer place, but that can't be true, sir,
can it? "

" All right, you can take the trap home,"
and, without further remark, Sturton passed
through the gate and, followed by his companion, cantered towards the cover.

It was a curious sight, a bright spring
April morning, the very day on which to
bury the hunting season, a day on which

20*

one's red coat not only looked but felt all too
warm, a languid day, an inert day, one in
which you felt neither man, horse, nor
hound could be expected to do their best,
a day, to those gathered round Ballater
Gorse, on which it seemed a storm was im-
pending. The hounds had not yet arrived,
but there were two different groups gathered
about the cover, watching each other with
grave suspicion and lowering looks. On
the one side were the followers of the Harkhallow Hunt, clad in their pink, and looking
at the grim-visaged mob that confronted
them in such reckless, devil-may-care
fashion as Rupert's Cavaliers might have
worn on the eve of Naseby fight. On the
other, a crowd of uneducated peasants,
goaded to madness by the inflammatory
harangues of such pinchbeck patriots as
Carmody and Last.

These paid politicians, who earn their
miserable living by playing on the passions of

the people, always remind me of the old
story of the trumpeter who, when captured,
was so promptly condemned to death by the
king, which seemed to those around him
such very harsh justice, on which the
monarch defended his judgment by saying :

"Though the man wasn't to fight meant,
He deserved to be hanged for his heartless excitement,
Himself in the fray doing nothing at all."

An Irish M.P., undergoing three months'
imprisonment for preaching sedition, rends
the very heavens with his cries for justice on
his persecutors, albeit his sentence and in-
carceration is probably limited to that time.
In less favoured countries, the political
agitator who seeks to pitchfork himself into
office by preaching the overthrowing of things
as they are, is apt to reap some years' imprisonment as his reward. Still he don't
whimper about it after the manner of his
Hibernian brother.

Jack Blake and the men clustered round

him had no earthly doubt that the mob
meant mischief, that the peasantry turned out
in considerable numbers for the crack meet
was well known to them, but they were not
given to muster in such numbers as were
present to-day, nor were they wont to hang
together with a sullen scowl on their brows,
and not endeavour to mingle with the gentlemen of the Hunt. In former days it had
been—"God save yer honour. Shure the bay
horse looks as if the day would be neither
too fast or too long for him," or "Glory be to
God, I niver saw yerself and the black mare
lookin' betther,—'twill be rale murther if ye
don't get a gallop to-day."

Blake, Power, and some of the leading
men of the hunt, were in animated conversation as the two officers rode up.

"It's unlucky," exclaimed Blake, "they
might have let us finish the season peace-
ably, but these fellows mean a row. I can
see McDermot is amongst them. It's a pity.

The ladies from Rathkelly will no doubt arrive with the hounds, and most likely Ratcliffe Eyre will be out himself."

"But McDermot is neither owner nor tenant of the Gorse, nor the land surrounding it, is he?" enquired Sturton, who had just come up in time to hear the speaker's last words.

"No," said Blake; "but I don't think that will make much difference. These fellows mean business and won't trouble their heads much about whether they have a *right* to interfere or not."

"That being the case, I should stand no nonsense," replied Sturton.

"That's just what will come to pass," replied Power, laughing. "I'm afraid the result will be unsatisfactory. A free fight, half a score of hounds more or less injured, and no sport."

"There'll be only one consolation," said Blake, laughing. "We can't be summoned this time. By the way, Sturton, I don't see him just now, but there was a fellow amongst the crowd there who ought to interest you, and that is Mike Cassidy."

" Ah !" said Sturton ; " the blackguard who meant to have unhorsed me on Callow-town race-course. I should like to have a good look at him."

" Here come the hounds," cried Chester, " and Mr. Eyre is with them himself."

" That settles it," observed Power. " It was not likely, but just possible, if he had not been out, they might have let us draw the cover. Now there'll be a fight for it. I'm sorry Mrs. Blake is out."

" My wife is a Galway girl," said Blake grimly, " and has heard the rattle of the sticks before now ; but, for all that, I wish she and the other ladies were at home."

It was quite evident, from the stern ex-pression of Mr. Eyre's face, that he had either had due notice of what was before him or

that he already grasped the situation. He
rode up and saluted his friends, and it was
clear at once, as those who knew him best felt
it would be, that he had no intention of yielding without a blow to the hostile demonstration. Looking at his watch, he said, "Time's
up. We'll give the laggards ten minutes'
grace, gentlemen, and then we'll draw."

As he finished speaking, McDermot,
accompanied by a bodyguard of half-a-dozen
strapping young fellows, came forward and
exclaimed in stentorian tones:

"We warn yez, Misther Eyre, we'll have
no more o' this. We're toired of you an'
your dogs, an' your friends. Hurroo, bhoys!
down with landlords and fox-hunting!"

"I have come to hunt," rejoined Ratcliffe
Eyre, in clear, resolute tones, "and I mean to
do it. You've not the slightest right to interfere with us, and if you do, you must take
the consequences, and perhaps get a worse
headache than you got last time."

"Maybe yerself won't come off so aisy to-day. As for the law, it's moighty little satisfaction we got out of it last toime. We'll take it into our own hands to-day. Ye've been warned, and the whole pack of yez had best take yerselves off at onest. There's those amongst us have purty long accounts to settle with some o' ye."

"Do you think, you scoundrel, that I'll be dictated to by you as to whether I hunt or don't hunt? As I've told you before, this is not your land, and you interfere with us at your peril! Throw in the hounds, O'Reilly."

The crowd of peasantry had gradually edged up to its advanced deputation, and there was an ugly gripping of sticks and a thrusting of hands into pockets in search of the stones with which most of them were lined, when like a "bolt from the blue," Katie Eyre, mounted on Rory, dashed in between the contending parties. Till this she had been with the other ladies in the background, whilst all the men of the hunt were clustered about her father.

" What do you mean by this ? " she exclaimed. " Haven't your fathers, aye, and your grandfathers, run, cheered, and in the good times ridden to, the Harkhallow Hounds ? What better friends to the sport were there ever than the peasantry all round Callowtown ? Where are the cowards that urge you on to this ? Not here, I am quite sure," she cried, with a mocking laugh. " Messrs. Last and Carmody have too much regard for their precious skins to be at the head of you now ! "

" By Jove," muttered Sturton to himself, " that girl looks positively handsome." And Katie was a figure fair to gaze upon. as she sat there, with head erect, her usually pale cheeks flushed with excitement, and her blue eyes flashing defiance upon her opponents.

" Go back, miss," growled one of the men

fiercely, "we don't want to hurt you or the other ladies."

"And that's just what you do," rejoined Katie. "What right have you to interfere with our day's pleasure, because a coward from over the water tells you to do so?"

"Toimes are changed," rejoined the hoarse voice of McDermot. "We've done with the Eyres of Rathkelly, with the Blakes, and the Powers, who have been suckin' the life-blood out of us intirely for years."

"Go back, Katie, at once," said her father, sternly—so sternly indeed as she had never yet known him to speak to her. "You have no business to leave your sister. Blake, you had best tell your wife and the other ladies to ride back to Rathkelly."

"All right," was the reply. "I'll be back in time for the fun, never fear. Come along, Katie. What a general you would make!" And so saying, he took hold of Rory's bridle and turned him towards the rear.

Katie threw one imploring glance at her father, but a most emphatic "Go!" burst from Mr. Eyre's lips, and in another minute or so she had rejoined Mrs. Blake and her sister.

"Mrs. Belton," exclaimed Blake, as he rode up, " your father has sent me to tell you to ride home at once, and Jennie, you must ride back to Rathkelly with them."

" Ah! Jack you *will* take care of yourself ? " exclaimed pretty little Mrs. Blake, who, in spite of having been born a Galway girl, was still not equal to contemplating a proximate chance of her husband's head being broken with that stoicism he had given her credit for.

"Don't you be frightened, little woman ; they won't hurt me, though perhaps I shall hurt one or two of them. As for Katie here, if she had only been a bit stronger, I'm not sure we shouldn't have kept her with us, but Eyre's orders are imperative, Mrs. Belton, and you really are much better out of the way."

"I suppose so," said Gracie. She had not been a soldier's wife for eight years without knowing what it was to have her husband ordered on the war-path, and knew that at such times women had best do as they are told and restrain their feelings.

"We shall be very anxious till we see you all back at Rathkelly," she continued, and turning her horse's head, she rode slowly back towards the highway, followed by Mrs. Blake and Katie.

That their day's sport would be ruined the gentlemen thought was most probable. Even if they succeeded in finding a fox, the probability was that he would be mobbed by the excited crowd round the cover, but they were determined not to give in without a fight for it, and being mounted and armed with their hunting crops, considered them-selves quite a match for the sticks of their opponents. But there was one factor they never dreamt of being used against them, and that was—stones! In the beautiful grass meadows that surrounded the cover, no one could certainly have expected the appearance of such missiles, but the greater part of the mob had arrived with their pockets fairly filled, and some of them had even gone so far as to bring small bags of these primitive projectiles. No sooner were the hounds thrown into cover than McDermot and his party let fly a volley of stones at their mounted adversaries, hitting a few of both men and horses.

For a moment the gentlemen were taken aback, and then Ratcliffe Eyre's voice rang out even above the yells of his opponents: "Charge the scoundrels home!" he cried, and setting spurs to his horse, he set the example by riding straight at McDermot. But that worthy, after the experience he had had on his own farm, had, in conjunction with

Cassidy, devised new tactics. As the horsemen neared them they broke and fled in all
directions, but only for a little distance, and
then turned and resumed their stoning with
greater vigour than ever. They were most
impartial in the distribution of their missiles,
hurling them at either hound or horseman, as
they got the opportunity, and the consequence
was that bruises and ugly blows became rife
amongst the gentlemen, while, as Jack Blake
pathetically expressed it afterwards, "it was
mighty hard for us even to get a clip at the
blackguards!"

Amongst those who distinguished themselves prominently on the side of the red-coats
were both Blake and Eyre, but the most
vengeful horsemen of them all, and the one
whose hunting crop, perhaps, did heaviest
execution, was Harold Sturton. Had he
known Mike Cassidy by sight, it might have
gone hard with that worthy, but the glance he
had had of him during the race had been so

transient that he could not be sure of his man.
It must not be supposed that McDermot's
followers did not turn pretty fiercely
upon their assailants when driven to bay,
and use their sticks pretty vigorously, but
the horsemen as a rule had the best of it at
close quarters. Still, as the battle proceeded,
it was evident that the gentlemen were getting
the worst of it. Contusions and bleeding
heads were rife amongst them. The blood is
streaming from the head of the Master of
Rathkelly. Jack Blake's face shows a heavy
bruise on it, whilst young Chester, although
he is only aware that he has been hit heavily
in the side with a stone, is riding with a
broken rib. Such few hounds as had showed
themselves outside the cover were mostly
crippled, when suddenly comes from the
far edge of the gorse a yell, and a cheery
" Gone away," in O'Reilly's voice. The fox
has broke, and with three or four couple of
hounds close upon his heels, speeds away

amidst a volley of stones to more secluded
quarters. One or two of his immediate
attendants utter dismal yelps as the missiles
strike them. Another second and the
huntsman blunders out of the gorse into the
field, and—fatal mistake!—pauses for a
moment to " blow 'em away." Crash ! comes a
volley of stones, one of which strikes him so
violently in the abdomen that he turns sick
and faint, and is near falling from his saddle.
A savage yell of exultation shows that his foes
are aware that he is disabled, and half-a-dozen
men rush furiously forward to drag him
from his horse, but Sturton, Blake, and two
or three more charge rapidly to his rescue,
and for a few minutes the hunting crops deal
out grim punishment to their assailants, then
the gentlemen fall back upon their main body,
bearing off the wounded man with them.

" It's no use," exclaimed Power, " there's
a rare, straight-going fox, gone away with five
of your darlings, Eyre, close at his brush, as

for the remainder they are scattered far and wide."

" Yes, and not a soul with the leaders, except young Ted, the second whip," said Blake. We must give it up, Eyre. O'Reilly is so hurt he can hardly keep his saddle. His horn has been lost in the scrimmage, and as for the hounds God knows whether you'll ever see half of them again."

" And shan't want to, poor brutes," rejoined Ratcliffe Eyre sternly. " Thank you all for standing by me, and assisting, gentlemen, at the funeral of the Harkhallow Hunt ! "

And amidst the yells and jeers of their opponents, Eyre and his friends rode slowly away.

CHAPTER IV.

"AFTER THE BATTLE."

THERE was little conversation amongst the members of the Harkhallow when they regained the highway. Men who have had the worst of the fray are rarely talkative. and most of them bore more or less marks of the conflict. Two of their number, indeed, were suffering considerably; a stone had cut Ratcliffe Eyre's head open, and he had lost a good deal of blood; the excitement had kept him going at the time, but he was beginning to feel weak and somewhat dazed now, and was glad to take a pull from a flask, which was proffered him. O'Reilly, too, was in great pain and in much distress about his hounds being scattered far and wide and he unable even to attempt to get them together again. Ratcliffe Eyre's words, too, had a gloomy significance, when he told them they had been present at the funeral of the Harkhallow Hunt. It was not the mere threat of an angry man, a hasty decision that he might be probably induced to reconsider, but they all knew that if the people, in obedience to the mandates of the League, maintained the attitude they had assumed that morning, neither Ratcliffe Eyre nor anyone else could hunt hounds in that country again.

"Good bye, Eyre, old man," exclaimed Power, "I turn off here. I hope you will be none the worse for that clip over the head to-morrow. You've lost more blood than is good for any of us as we get on in life. Take my advice, leave 'the matarials' alone to-night and stick to the claret."

By twos and threes the party fell off, till at last there were only those bound for Rathkelly left riding together.

"It was a mighty pretty fight while it lasted," remarked the irrepressible Blake to Sturton, by whose side he was riding. "It was the stones that beat us. Who would have thought of the spalpeens filling their pockets with them before they came to Ballater Gorse? As for that villain McDermot, he was like an eel, all over the place, and, hard though I tried, I never succeeded in getting a crack at him. Did you come across your friend Cassidy?"

"I'm afraid not," rejoined the other. "I hit out pretty hard at a good many of them, in the hope that I might be settling that little debt I owe him, but I'm bound to say I came across no face that reminded me of the man I saw at the brook."

"Ah, the thief," rejoined Blake, laughing, "his head is still tender from that welt of Ryan's stick. He'd be a little shy of putting it in danger this morning."

"I suppose," said Sturton, "what Eyre

said is about the case; we have attended the very last meet of the Harkhallow?"

"Not a doubt about it," replied Blake, as his face fell. "It's a beautiful country, and, oh, dear! what a lot of fun I've had in it, but it's all over now. Great heavens! fancy the country without hunting!"

"And without the money spent in it that a well-done pack represents," rejoined Sturton drily.

On arrival at Rathkelly they found the ladies in a state of great anxiety, which the appearance of the little cavalcade was not calculated to allay.

Mr. Eyre indeed looked worn and ghastly, and the blood-stained handkerchief which had been bound round his head at a wet ditch they happened to pass on their way home, had by no means tended to improve his appearance.

The huntsman, too, was palpably in great pain; and, in spite of his protestations, Mrs.

Blake viewed with dismay a very ugly bruise on her husband's cheek.

Tom Chester was also very pale, although he steadily declined to admit that he had received more than a "crack in the ribs." Mrs. Belton at once took command of her father.

"Get him to bed as quick as you can," said [Sturton, "and I'll send Conolly over as soon as I get back."

"But surely you're not going home? You and Mr. Chester must stay here for the night after all this turmoil," rejoined Mrs. Belton.

"Ten thousand thanks—no. I shall be doing better service in the way I mention; besides, Chester won't admit he's hurt, but I know he is in great pain." And then Sturton turned to say good-bye to the others.

"It's the most disgraceful business ever heard of," flamed forth Miss Eyre. "And I suppose, in such a turmoil as that, no one could see whose hand it was threw that stone at my father?"

"No, I don't think any of us could tell you that."

"You seem to be the only one of the party that has escaped without injury, Captain Sturton. How was that?"

"Well, perhaps it was luck, or perhaps it was prudence. I didn't put myself so prominently forward as Miss Eyre."

She gave a contemptuous toss of her head.

"Why will he always treat me like a child?" she muttered. "No, Captain Sturton," she said with supreme disdain. "I *do* know better than that. I know very well you were in the front of the fight. *You* take care of yourself—*nonsense!*"

"Then I suppose it was luck," replied Sturton, acknowledging Miss Eyre's compliment by a mocking bow. "And now we must really say good-bye, for I've promised

to send Conolly to see your father at once.
It's just as well a doctor should have a look
at him. I don't suppose he wants anything
more than keeping quiet, but it's as well to
be on the safe side."

Another minute and he and Chester had
swung themselves into their saddles, though
the slight spasm that shot across the latter's
face showed the trifling effort cost him some
pain.

"I'm afraid you caught a nasty one in the
ribs, Tom," said Sturton, as the pair turned
out of the Rathkelly gates. "As for me,
although I'm not marked externally, I'm
bruised all over. Smart idea of the beggars
to have those stones. Well! we've had our
last day's hunting in Ireland, and I daresay
you think it's as well."

"My side is rather painful," replied Chester;
"but wasn't Miss Eyre splendid? By Jove,
she looked a girl to die for!"

"She did look rather well," said Sturton,

" and showed pluck. I never even thought her good-looking before."

" Good-looking," repeated Chester, " why I think she is the prettiest girl I ever saw."

" All right, Tom," said the other, laughing, " but you see you're quite gone about her, and I'm not. By Jove! here's a bit of luck. Here's Conolly. How are you doctor ? "

" Flourishing like a bay tree," replied the doctor, " which, it strikes me, is more than you are, Mr. Chester. I heard from a fellow I met on the road that there had been the divil's own row at Ballater Corse, and that there were cracked crowns lying around thick as blackberries in autumn. Is it thrue ? "

" It is so," replied Sturton, " there has been about the freest fight that ever you saw. There's plenty of work for you, doctor, but in the first instance, I want you to go straight to Rathkelly. Mr. Eyre has got his head cut open, and poor O'Reilly, I'm afraid, is even more seriously hurt."

"All right! I'll be there in a jiffey; one moment, can I do anything for either of you before I go?"

"No, thanks," replied Chester, "I shall do very well till I get to barracks."

"Ah! and there of course your own surgeons will look after you," said Conolly, and the doctor put his horse into a smart canter and disappeared.

McDermot and Cassidy were in ecstasies at their triumph. True, many of their followers had been roughly handled by the gentlemen, but the leaders of the mob had been as sparing of their persons as those who had counselled the boycotting of the hounds, and Messrs. Carmody and Last were strongly of opinion that they owed it to their constituents to take great care of themselves. Both McDermot and Cassidy, more especially the latter, were animated by a spirit of vengeance, and the two men harangued their followers, and urged them to do their work thoroughly.

" Show 'em you're in earnest, bhoys," roared
Cassidy, " and don't let a dog of the pack ever
get back to Rathkelly," and the excited
peasantry, inflamed to madness by the violent
speeches they had lately listened to, and
intoxicated by their success, spread about
the country, killing or mutilating every luckless hound they could lay hands upon.

The Indians of the Far West inflict
nameless tortures on their enemies when
they fall into their hands, but they do not
extend their animosity to dumb creatures.
As for the second whip, he was a plucky
young fellow, and had received short but
decisive orders from the huntsman before the
hounds were thrown into cover.

" Bear in mind, Ted," said that functionary,
" that yez has nothing to do with the row.
Get away with the hounds if you can, and
stick to them." And Ted had strictly obeyed
orders, to the utter neglect of his more
legitimate functions, and finally, after a

rattling gallop of some three or four miles,
during which the three couple of hounds he
had with him were always very close upon
their fox, pulled him down in the open.

The final ceremonies over, Ted bethought
himself of what he was to do next. There
wasn't a soul with him, and from what he
had seen he felt sure that there would be
no further hunting that day. Clearly he
thought his duty was to pick up as many
hounds as he possibly could, and make the
best of his way back to Rathkelly; and with
this object he commenced blowing his horn,
but if a few stray hounds heard him, so did
a good many half-maddened peasants, and it
speedily became palpable to the lad, that
unless he used considerable discretion, neither
he nor the hounds with him would ever reach
Rathkelly that night, nor, as far as the hounds
were concerned, probably ever reach Rathkelly at all. He was none too soon, for the
peasantry were craftily hemming him in, and

without more ado he started with such hounds as he had at his heels, and struck out straight for the Castle, where he eventually arrived with a mere remnant of the pack that had left it in the morning.

It was the last day of the Harkhallow Hunt, and neither horn nor hound have been heard in that country since.

CHAPTER V.

It was a gala night in the House of Commons.
The most eminent orator of the age has risen
early in the evening, and, though once more
for over an hour and a half his audience hung
entranced upon his utterances, demonstrated
that language is given us to conceal our
thoughts.   More explicit than usual, upon
this occasion he is supposed to admit that
law and order in England and law and
order in Ireland are by no means the same
thing, and furthermore vaguely suggests that
of two evils it is better to choose the less,
and to submit to robbery without resistance
for fear murder should come of it, forgetting
that meek submission to anarchy and

deference to the clamour of windy mob orators, is only characteristic of nations in their decadence.

Dan Carmody has distinguished himself as usual in the course of the evening by audibly alluding to the Government as " a set of Tory skunks," a flower of language which had nearly procured him the honour of being named by the Speaker, his escape being due to the fact that those who called him to order, though positive that the term came from the Irish benches, were not quite sure as to who was the actual delinquent.

Mr. Last had already made his *debut* in the House, and demonstrated that the Honourable Member for Callowtown was a fluent speaker of the old conventional type. His oration might be described as froth, fizzle, and inter-minable.

" Sort of fellow to whom the new Closure rules seem peculiarly adapted," was the criticism of the Honourable Augustus

Danby, as he strolled out of the room to
soothe his feelings with a cigar. "Regular
boot-eater, that fellow, no doubt."

"What the deuce do you mean, 'Gus?"
inquired one of his intimates.

"Been studying up this Irish question,
don't you know?" rejoined the Honourable
Augustus—"gone through a regular course
of Lever's novels; know all about

> 'The finest pisantry on a fruitful sod,
> Fighting like divils for conciliation,
> And hating each other for the love of God.'

A boot-eater up in the Far West means a jury-
man who will dine off those useful articles
before he assents to any verdict but his own.
Should think Last is that sort of fellow."

The Honourable Augustus Danby was a
capital type of a certain class in the House
of Commons. He never spoke himself. He
often wondered how the deuce fellows could
have so much to say about a thing! Was
wont to asseverate, "Never knew a fellow

who talked much who did anything. Look
at a street row," he continued, philosophi-
cally, " whenever they talk much they don't
fight. A Johnnie who brags awfully about
his hunting or shooting in the smoking-room
over night, you never hear much of the next
day. Don't understand it myself, but think
we should get on a good deal quicker if we
had a good deal less jaw."

The Honourable Augustus Danby might
not be very clever, but at the same time
there is a very large proportion of educated
people outside the House of Commons who
are coming very much to his way of
thinking.

" Bedad! me bhoy," said Dan Carmody, as
he entered the smoking-room shortly afterwards with James Last, " you fetched 'em.
If it hadn't been for the cussed rules these
murthering Tories have passed, you'd have
knocked 'em silly ! "

" It's a shame, Dan, I tell ye. If it hadn't

2 2 *

been for that midnight closure business, I
could have gone on aisily till two. Will we
get Home Rule, do ye think?"

Dan Carmody closed his right eye signifi-
cantly, as, hailing a passing waiter, he demanded "six of Irish hot."

"Home Rule!" he said. "What do we
want with it? Isn't this good enough for ye?
The pay is dacent, and the place is moighty
convanient for a gintleman to take his chop
in and enjoy himself. Home Rule—God
forbid! This place is good enough for me
anny way."

"Well, I'm satisfied," said Mr. Last. "But
won't they be expectin' something the other
side St. George's Channel?"

"Not they. Shure, payin' no rint is good
enough for thim. We'll get our orders from
New York, or else maybe they'll send a few
bhoys across to get up another dynamite
scare. As for the people in Ireland, they've
been expecting the Millennium ever since I

can recollect; and the bigger orders you draw upon their imagination, the more the poor divils believe in you."

"Slow work this," said Mr. Danby to his confidential friend; "think politics a mistake myself. Think I shall turn 'em up as soon as this Parliament is kicked out. They were before my time, but can't understand what made fellows like Palmerston, Lord Derby, and Lord George Bentinck take to this sort of thing; and talk about the best club in London, why if any of the Johnnies at the Heliotrope used the sort of language that the chaps here habitually use to each other, why, dash it all! they would be cast out of the community!"

"Come on, 'Gus," replied his friend, laughing, "we will go down to the Heliotrope, and see how they're betting on the Guineas."

And with that, these two distinguished senators left the house, and hailed the nearest hansom.

The Honourable Augustus Danby, a younger son of the Earl of Rottondene, had been pitchforked into a borough through the family interest, not in the least because he aspired to take a part in the government of his country, but simply because the borough of Cracksley always had been held by a scion of the Rottondene family.

As the Honourable Augustus was totally dependent upon his noble father, and had manifested neither disposition nor ability to earn his own living, he naturally acquiesced in the paternal mandate; but the whole thing was, to him, a blank and inexplicable mystery. He voted straight enough with his party; he never troubled the House with his own eloquence; and it was ever a source of astonishment to him how the deuce a fellow could have so much to say.

As the two young men entered the smoking-room of the Heliotrope, Danby's eye was caught by a slight, dark man, who, with his back to the fire, was recounting an adventure of some sort to the two or three men seated round it.

"You must have had a lively morning," remarked one of his auditors.

"Rather," was the reply. It was about the hottest time I ever had in the country ; and they make it pretty lively for us soldiers, too, during the elections."

"Hulloa, Sturton !" exclaimed Danby, "why, I haven't seen you for ages ! "

"No," rejoined the other, as he shook hands. " I'm a soldier on the other side St. George's Channel. And pretty dull work it is. I was just telling these fellows that the League, in its wisdom, has put down hunting in the part I come from, and simply stoned us all, hounds included, out of the field last time we met."

"Rum go, that; always understood the Irish were about the most sporting people out."

"So they are," rejoined Sturton, "if they were only let alone. However, I think the League is getting towards the end of its tether. Of course, it'll die hard. These fellows would sooner go spouting about the country than work for their living."

"Yes," remarked Danby. "I've always noticed that the ' friends of the people' have a great dislike to work, and to soap and water."

Sturton laughed, as he replied, "You don't quite understand it.

' If loving the people is Canaan in view,
  It's Canaan, paid quarterly, to have 'em love you.'

But what are you people doing here?"

"If you mean at Westminster," said Danby, "it's the same old game. Eminent politicians in opposition, anxiously demonstrating how much better they could govern the country than our fellows. Eminent politicians in office, quite satisfied with the way they do it themselves, and quite determined not to give them a chance if they can help it.

" What a minister you'll make, when your time comes," said Sturton.

" None of your chaff, Harold," replied the senator. " Could have given them a wrinkle, though, the other night. They go taxing all sorts of things which cost quite enough money as it is. If they'd only tax talk and bad language, we should contribute pretty handsomely to the revenue down at St. Stephen's."

" Well, we shouldn't get much out of you, at all events," rejoined Sturton.

" No," replied Danby placidly. " I'm that blessing to my country—a silent member. Come over for long ? "

" I've got a month's leave," said Sturton, " but the regiment is coming across in a few weeks ; Portsmouth, or Aldershot, I believe, being our destination."

Sturton had left Conroy, indeed, about a week after assisting at what its master aptly termed "the funeral of the Harkhallow Hunt." Mrs. Belton, who had postponed her departure for a few days on account of her father's injuries, had gladly accepted his escort to London. Mr. Eyre was pronounced by Conolly pretty well himself again before Grace left, but she saw clearly that life at Rathkelly was about to become very hard for her father and sister, and, indeed, all their neighbours; about the suppression of the League there could be no eventual doubt.

Ratcliffe Eyre, indeed, might well take a gloomy view of the situation. Although a little shaken, about a week saw him thoroughly recovered from the blow on his head. If it was a severe blow to his vanity to give up the hounds, yet in somewise the excuse was opportune. He was not the sort of man to have a goodly balance at his banker's, and money was beginning to be

very short with Mr. Eyre. He had publicly
announced his abandonment of the Harkhallow country, and within a week the débris
of his pack, and nearly all the horses, had
been despatched to Dublin for sale, Rory,
a driving horse, and his own hack being all
he had retained out of his numerous stud.

"Well, papa," said Katie, "the fun was
about over for this year, but how we're to
get on next season I'm sure I don't know.
Just fancy Rathkelly without hunting! The
Blakes, too, talk seriously of going away.
Mr. Blake says they have stopped hunting,
and he has no doubt they'll take the shooting
into their own hands immediately; and, as
he says, it's no fun living in a country where
all amusements are prohibited."

"We must just make the best of things,
Katie," replied Mr. Eyre. "Times are very
hard for us all round, but I shall get on very
well with my people if the League don't come
between us. As for that fellow Cassidy, he is

a bitter, bad lot; and out he goes as soon as his time is up."

"I never liked them, papa, neither himself nor his wife; and Norah tells me that he is making a deal of mischief about the country."

A still steady and constant visitor at Rathkelly was Tom Chester; and if persistent devotion could serve a man in such case, he deserved to succeed. Mrs. Belton had been sorely tempted to once more plead his cause with her wilful sister, but prudence at last prevailed. " We have already quarrelled over it," she said to herself, "and I declared I would never allude to the subject again. I shouldn't so much mind about that, but I honestly believe that I should do Mr. Chester no service by pressing his cause. Katie is missing a chance which most likely won't come to her again."

It is rather a waste of time to advocate the claims of one man for favourable consideration when a young lady happens to be

in love with another. But Grace had no
suspicion of her sister's infatuation for
Sturton. There certainly was not much to
indicate any feeling of that kind between the
pair. Sturton never had paid her any
marked attention, and invariably treated her
as a school-girl, whom he had known from
a child. Grace remembered her sister a
hot-tempered little girl of eight or nine;
she regarded her now as a girl still possessed
of a rather uncontrollable temper, and much
spoiled from want of control and guidance.
Norah could have enlightened her as to the
real state of affairs, but then Katie confided a
good deal more to her foster-sister than she
did to Grace. It is true that Katie had never
even whispered her secret to Norah, but the
girl was far too quick witted not to discover
her young mistress's passion for Harold
Sturton, carefully concealed in her own
breast though she might deem it. Poor
Katie! to the very last Mrs. Belton was

destined to arouse her jealousy. She was, of course, aware that Grace travelled to London under Sturton's escort.

"It's disgraceful," she exclaimed. "Quite an arranged thing. She ought to be ashamed of herself. A married woman. I only wish her husband knew," and then this stern young moralist whimpered a little, and bitterly lamented that she was not in Mrs. Belton's place!

CHAPTER VI.

Tim Ryan and Terence are both now marked men in the barony. They both steadfastly refuse to join the League and are already subject to various menaces on that point. They have been both warned that if they do not obey its dictates it will be the worse for them, and—spurred on by commands from America—the League has been unusually active around Callowtown of late. The Council in New York are insisting that they must have more to show for their money. They do not consider that the reign of terror which has been established is being carried out with sufficient severity. Examples must be made of those who refuse compliance with the mandates of the League,

and Messrs. Last and Carmody have in consequence been delivering still more inflammatory harangues, if possible, than before. A
stringent No-rent manifesto has been issued,
and solemn warning given that any infringement of this command will be visited heavily
on the culprit.

" What's Misther Last got to do with my
paying my rint? that's a thing between me
and the Masther. He's taken a good bit
off, and though times are hard I can manage
to pay yet, glory be to God ! And to think of
their stopping the hunting ! I never thought
to see the day when the bhoys would stone
the hounds, the dumb craythurs ! "

" Mike Cassidy is one of the worst of the
lot. He's never forgiven us for that day on
the race-course, when the black-hearted thief
tried to stop Miss Katie's horse."

" Ah! 'twas a gay afternoon that," said
Ryan, laughing; " it was a swate bit of a
scrimmage while it lasted, it just gave a flavour

to the whisky afterwards, and then Rory won
afther all."

" 'Twas a mighty pleasant day," replied
Terence, with a smile, as he thought of what
a fuss his sweetheart had made with him, for
Norah, after she had once got over her
dismay at his cracked crown, thought she
couldn't make too much of her lover after
the staunch way in which he had stood by
her father. " That's a nice lot of beasts you
picked up last market day."

" 'Deed, and they are," rejoined the farmer.
" Keep is scarce the other side Callowtown.
They are a bit low in flesh, but they will soon
come round on my grass land."

" Divil a fear of that! Everyone knows
yours is the best grass farm in the barony,
Mr. Ryan."

" It's good land! It's good land!" said
the farmer complacently, " and, Terence, I
got the bastes a rale bargain. I'll turn a
bit of money over that lot."

" Well! threatened men live long," remarked Terence, " and as for Mike Cassidy,
he may bluster a good deal, but I don't think
he'll dare meddle with either of us."

" At all events," replied Ryan, " we are
not going to be tould what we are to do by
the likes of Mike Cassidy. I did hear though,"
he continued, dropping his voice, " that Mike
had joined the Moonlighters."

" I believe that's so," rejoined Terence,
" the cowardly brutes, who have no idea of
the fun of a rale fight."

But, though Terence Flynn spoke in this
light-hearted, careless fashion, he was quite
aware that things were looking rather serious
for both himself and Ryan. He knew that
there was an organised force of Moonlighters
sworn to do the bidding of the League, and
though their identity was kept a profound
secret, there were several young men on the
country side who were suspected of belonging
to the association, and, amongst others, Mike

Cassidy. Several outrages had been reported
of late as the work of these midnight visitors,
and though Terence was as daring a young
fellow as might be, still, what chance had a
man who was suddenly set upon by eight or
ten others, all armed? It seemed intolerable
to him that a stranger like Mr. Last, whom
they had never even seen till a few months ago,
should come here, to Callowtown, and interfere between the county gentlemen and their
tenants.

Those who joined the League had to
contribute to its support, and — as far as
Terence made out—to pay such men as
Carmody for meddling in their private affairs;
and yet he knew, in defiance of the law, that
the League had retaliated brutally on those
who had refused to join it.

It was a beautiful spring morning when—
a few days after the above conversation—
Farmer Ryan emerged from his cabin door,
and took a long breath of the delicious soft

23*

air, which already brought a savour of the coming summer.

" Gran' weather, after the rain, Mary," he shouted back into the house. " It will bring the grass on apace, we shall have it over our ankles before we know where we are. I'll just slip up, my woman, to the top field, and have a look at the bastes." And with that, and blithely whistling " The Hare in the Corn," Tim Ryan strode gaily along up to his best bit of pasture. When he reached the gate he stopped aghast, and a savage execration escaped his lips.

" My poor bastes; shure the divils needn't have tortured *you* for not joining the League! " and, opening the gate, he passed through, and with eyes sparkling with anger and grief, contemplated his nine unfortunate bullocks tailless and bleeding, but that was not the sole extent of the mischief that had been wrought in the night, for Mary Ryan's two milch cows lay helplessly houghed besides.

" The wife will be real mad when she hears Eileen and Kathleen, the two best milkers about here, are as good as dead, for there's nothing left now but to put the poor craythurs out of their misery."

Tim Ryan was right ; when he got home and told the wife his news, she at first burst into tears at the loss of her pets, but this was followed by a storm of invectives, chiefly levelled at Mike Cassidy.

Of course, Tim would go to the poliss! A murthering scoundrel like that was not to go about unpunished, she hoped, indade there was no use in having prisons, if the likes of him were not to be put in thim! Did Tim mane to bate the blackguard himself? She would give him a bit of her mind next time she met him ! Ah, may be let him feel the weight of her hand besides !

" It's him, the thief, that's at the bottom of it, I've no doubt; but he'll swear he knows nothing about it. And, I doubt, we'll not

manage to bring it home to him! No fear,
but what I'll thry, Mary ; 'deed, and if I can't
take the law on him, sure I can give him a
bating *because he didn't do it!*"

The news of the mutilation of Ryan's cattle
spread rapidly through the district, and there
was considerable popular sympathy evoked
on his behalf. It was whispered about that
Cassidy knew something of it. But, for all
that, no one would come forward and testify
to such knowledge. There could be little
doubt that the perpetrators of the outrage
were pretty well known all through the
country side. Still it was well known that
any one who came forward and gave information would be a marked man, and the
terrorism of the League was so dreaded
that honest men feared to incur its dis-
pleasure.

Ratcliffe Eyre, in his double capacity of
landlord and magistrate, was especially active
in his endeavours to trace out the offenders.

He would have done so in any case, but the
fact that Mike Cassidy was supposed to be
one of them gave additional zest to the
pursuit. With this recalcitrant tenant the
Master of Rathkelly had vowed to have a
stern day of reckoning. He knew he was a
prominent member of the League. He had
seen him amongst the mob that shouted for
Mr. Last at the Callowtown election. He had
seen him prominent amongst the boycotters
of the Harkhallow Hunt. He certainly could
not prove that it was Cassidy's hand that
fired that shot at him on his way home from
Callowtown, but Ratcliffe Eyre had no doubt
in his own mind that it was so. He was
equally convinced of Cassidy's guilt on this
occasion, and offered a liberal reward to any
one who would come forward and give
evidence which might lead to the conviction
of the offenders. But the peasantry remained
silent, and, despite the Master of Rathkelly's
firm belief that the names of the Moonlighters

were well known, he could get no information concerning them.

Katie, who inherited in some measure her father's passionate and overbearing disposition, which her bringing-up had still further tended to foster, was furious at the .dastardly outrage.

" I wouldn't have Cassidy another hour on the estate, papa, if I were you."

" I won't, my dear," rejoined her father. " I must have him there till his notice expires. I'd have him in gaol this minute if I could only get evidence against him."

Threats break no bones, and in such matters as this the secrets of the League were well kept. When it came to assassination the saving of their own skins usually led to considerable desire to turn informer amongst most of those concerned.

But the days slip by, and though the people bowed to the decision of the League—more especially as regarded the non-payment of rent

—yet they did not subscribe to the support of
that patriotic institution in the manner that the
leaders of the movement had hoped for. The
Council in New York, for instance, expressed
themselves very much disgusted that these
unregenerate Irishmen contributed so sparely
to the funds necessary to procure the freedom
of their country. They grumbled ominously,
and declared that four-fifths of the money that
supported the movement came from America.
" Nor," continued the Council, in a dispatch
sent to the chiefs of the Irish party, " are your
acts equal to your words. You make brave
speeches, but your followers don't act up to
them; brave words, but we want substan-
tiality. We must have something stronger
than the mutilation of cattle. *Strike home!*
and let us hear that you have rid yourselves
of some of your persecutors. Make the
authority of the League thoroughly respected!
It ought to be made clear that the man who
fails to join the League carries his life in his

hand. See to this, and see to it speedily, or
we must send over men more fitted for the
work."

And so the speeches of Irish members got
more and more inflammatory. Moonlighters
were organised over many parts of the
country, and the subordinate chiefs of the
League got the significant hint *to strike terror
into the hearts of their oppressors.* But,
unfortunately, a marked change had come
over the state of affairs. The English
government was sternly determined to restore
law and order in Ireland, and though the
Council in New York might bluster, and the
Irish chiefs harangue—and go to prison for
so haranguing—more terror had been struck
into the hearts of the National League than
into those of the recognised guardians of law
and order. That there should be some defiant
expiring flickers was to be expected, but
there was to be seen looming in the future
an end to that profitable patriotism on which

men like Messrs. Carmody and Last had so bravely ruffled it for some time.

About a week after the outrage on his farm, Ryan happened to come across Cassidy on the road. He was about to pass him without speaking, not because they had fought at Callowtown, but for the reason that a bitter animosity had sprung up between the two men. Mike Cassidy was in the humour to enjoy the revenge, which, if he had not taken an actual part in, had been doubtless wreaked on Ryan at his instigation.

With a sneer on his face, he exclaimed in jeering tones :

"The top of the morning to you, Misther Ryan, sure it's foine weather for the grass, and there's the divil's own demand for ox-tails they tell me."

The blood rushed into Tim Ryan's head, and his eyes glittered with fury as he exclaimed :

" By my sowl, Mike Cassidy, if I only felt

shure ye'd done it, I'd bate the life out of ye
this minute! Be a man, now, and own up to
it if ye did! I'll swear not to take the law of
ye! We'll settle this quarrel betune our two
selves, here and now."

"Ah! what would I know about the
docking of yer bastes? Shure I heard of it
like everyone else. 'Dade it's just the talk of
the country side."

"There's a reckoning to come between you
and me, Mike Cassidy. I'll know the truth
about them cows some day, and look to
yerself if I find that you have had a hand
in it."

"Ye'd betther look to yerself," retorted the
other. "I tould you what would come of
going against the League, so don't blame me
for it. Look to yerself, me man, or worse
may come of it! We're going to stand no
more nonsense in these parts, and, as Misther
Last says, there's only two ways about it,
hem as is not for us is against us."

" To the divil with your National League ! What have I to do with a lot of strangers from across the wather, who come over here and pretend to manage our affairs for us ? More likely 'tis for what they can get, the blood-suckers ! " and Tim Ryan's fingers fairly itched as he gripped his stick tight and wished he'd some fair pretext for quarrelling with the other.

" I'll wish ye good morning, Misther Ryan," said Cassidy, with a bow of mock politeness. " I meant it friendly, and I can only hope ye'll not regret having quarrelled with the League."

And with a grin upon his face that very nearly brought Ryan's stick about his shoulders, Mr. Cassidy went on his way.

CHAPTER VII.

"THE MURDER OF RYAN."

McDermot was the head man of the branch
of the League that ruled in the Rathkelly
district, and a few days after Cassidy's
encounter with Ryan the former received
a summons to attend a meeting at McDermot's house, for the discussion of important
affairs which would be laid before them.
Cassidy was in high spirits at this. He was
in that frame of mind which would make
it a pleasure to wreak his spite on
nearly every man in the barony. He had
never been popular, and the part he had
taken of late as an adherent of the League
had still further conduced to his unpopularity.
The summons to McDermot's he knew was

the prelude to what he termed " business."
At a meeting there, as we know, the boycotting of the hounds had been determined
on, similarly at McDermot's house had gone
forth the fiat for the mutilation of Ryan's
cattle. It was quite blithely that Mike
Cassidy tramped up to McDermot's in
obedience to his chief's command. He
had many ends to gratify, and had little
doubt that something would be decided on
at this meeting which would serve his turn.
If he could stir the minds of this branch
council to take action against Terence Flynn,
he would do so. He hated Flynn as only
one man can hate another whom he regards
as possessing a secret of his, which carries a
noose at the end of it, and—although, as we
know erroneously—he believed Terence to
know more or less of his attempt on Mr.
Eyre's life. Hundreds of times had he
puzzled his brain to know what it was that
Terence had found in the road. Had he

known that it was simply a case of that con-
science "that doth make cowards of us all,"
that Terence had picked up nothing, he
would have been much surprised.

When they were all comfortably assembled
in McDermot's parlour, that gentleman rose,
and proceeded to inform them that the
orders of the League had been very im-
perfectly carried out in that neighbourhood,
and that nowhere had they been so badly
obeyed as in the Rathkelly barony. Michael
Cassidy was the only one of the council
who was a tenant of the tyrant Eyre, and
he intended to call on him to give information concerning his brother tenants on that
estate. The League had thought it necessary to
give orders that no further rents should be
paid to their oppressors, and—"Gentlemen!
ye'd have thought every wan would have
been only too happy to comply with such a
demand!"

Considerable applause from the half-score

members present, and a cry from Cassidy:
"The divil a ha'penny have *I* parted with
to the old nagur! but there's thim as has!"

"Now," continued McDermot, "we can't
have this going on! We gave that spalpeen
Ryan a hint the other night, that he'd betther
not go against the League, but begorrah! our
chief says this rint-paying must be put a stop
to! Hints seem no use. They say," and
here he lowered his voice, "we must *make
an example!*"

The laughter was at once stilled, and the
men's faces became grave, for what this meant
was only too patent to all of them. Still, men
who will torture dumb creatures have no moral
objection to murder. It resolves itself into
a sheer case of their own physical safety.
Cassidy's eyes gleamed and sparkled vindic-
tively. His opportunity had come. He was
about to be questioned as to which of the
Rathkelly tenants had paid their rents, and
nothing was easier than to denounce the

two men he most hated—Ryan and Terence
Flynn. In the case of the former he had
good grounds for saying so. The man had
gone direct to the agent, and there could
be no more reasonable conclusion, but with
Terence it was different. Most of the tenantry
believed he had, but it was pure conjecture.
He had been much more guarded in his
proceedings than Ryan, and if he had gone
to the agent's it had not been openly.

"Now, Cassidy," exclaimed McDermot,
"Who are *thim as has?*"

"Ryan has paid his rint, bad cess to him."

"You know this for certain," said
McDermot."

"Shure there isn't a bhoy in the barony
but what knows it."

"Who else?"

"Terence Flynn."

"And yez know this for shure?" once
again asked McDermot.

"It's not known loike the other, but I

know it. He is a sly fox, that Flynn, but by jabers he don't fool me."

And now came a low muttered conference between McDermot and his companions. The two farmers denounced by Cassidy had long been marked men by the League on account of their declining to join or subscribe to it, and gradually this Irish Vehmgericht came to the conclusion that, in accordance with the orders of their chief, no better example could be made than Timothy Ryan!—a well-to-do man, and an old tenant—and it was accordingly agreed amongst them that he should be "*visited*." This, in the mellifluous language of the League, meant murdered, or near akin to it.

"Now," said McDermot, "we'll do this of course in the regular fashion. I'll just write down the name of the bhoys for the job, and av course by our oath the names must never pass our lips. The bhoys then will each get their notice that they're wanted, and it would

be best they shouldn't know whose in it till
they're all mustered." McDermot then produced a pencil and a piece of paper, and
slowly and with much thought proceeded to
write down some half-score of names. His
labours were finished at last, and he then
passed the list round to his companions. It
so happened that the last man to receive the
list was Cassidy, and he could not suppress a
slight start as he saw his own name at the
top of it. 'Twas not that his thoughts
towards Ryan were not quite sufficiently
murderous, but somehow he had arrived at
the conclusion that he had done his share of
moonlighting work, that he had now got a
seat on the Branch Council, and could do
away with the objects of his dislike by
deputy, which had the advantage of being
equally efficacious, and very much safer.

"You don't seem to like the job," said
McDermot, "maybe it's afraid ye are?"

"Sorra a bit," replied Cassidy, "but faith!

I thought I'd done my share of moonlighting of late."

" So ye have, Mike! so ye have!" replied McDermot, "and right well ye've done it! But ye see we always pick the names pretty well from distant parts of the district, and we must have one man in who knows the ground and all about it. Now, no man knows Ryan's holding better than you."

" Thrue for ye, Misther McDermot! and there's nobody hates him worse in the whole barony."

" Bedad, ye're the very boy for the business!"

This illegal tribunal having thus briefly disposed of the life of one of their fellows, proceeded to pass the whiskey about and otherwise enjoy themselves. As they were leaving at the end of the entertainment, Cassidy took McDermot aside for one moment and whispered into his ear :

" Ye want no half measures, I suppose ? "

"We want an example, Mike; we have put it in your hands, and ye'll do what ye think best."

Mike Cassidy nodded, and as he strolled home, said to himself, "If I make an example this time, I'll take moighty good care I'll make another before long. I don't feel quite aisy whilst Terence Flynn is walking round."

Ryan was sitting moodily at supper with his wife, brooding over his heavy losses; they were in truth very considerable to a man of his station, and the badness of the times only made them more severely felt. He had paid his rent in defiance of the League, but much reduced though it was, yet it seemed a big sum of money to part with at present, and now on the top of it came the loss of the two cows. Suddenly there was a tap at the door, and on Mrs. Ryan unbolting it her daughter entered. Although formally appointed Miss Katie's maid, she constantly obtained leave to run up and visit her parents.

"How grave you look, father," she exclaimed as she kissed him.

"It's enough to make a man look grave, Norah, to have his stock trated as mine wor! It's hard work enough to get along without having your property desthroyed."

"Yes, indeed," exclaimed Mary Ryan; "between the times and the League, Lord knows what will become of us."

"I'd break every bone in that Cassidy's body," said the farmer savagely. "I'm sorry I didn't when I met the baste a few days back."

"Have you heard anything, father? Do you know for certain 'twas him? Have you any evidence that he was one of them? The Masther swears he'd put him in jail if he could only prove it against him."

"No," replied Ryan, "I can't prove it; but I'm as sure he'd a hand in it as there's a sun in Heaven! I suppose you're moighty quiet at the Castle now?"

"Yes; since Mrs. Belton left, and Captain Sturton went on leave, we have but few visitors. Mr. Chester comes oftener than anyone. He's moighty sweet on Miss Katie."

"And she?" inquired Mrs. Ryan eagerly, with all a woman's interest in a love affair.

"Doesn't care a snap of her fingers about him. It's a pity, for he's a fine-looking young man." And then the conversation drifted into desultory channels appertaining to the domestic of both Castle and cabin.

Norah's visit had cheered her parents up not a little. They had very few visitors now. They were not boycotted, but the neighbours were afraid to be intimate, and drop in on people who were under the ban of the League. Time slipped away, and when Norah rose to go, her mother suggested that she had better stay and sleep in her old room, little thinking what a terrible night the luckless girl was destined to pass. Ryan looked carefully to the fastenings of door and window before

they retired to rest. Since the mutilation of
his cattle, he had begun to take these precautions—things about which he had been
very careless previously. Another half-hour,
and the whole family were in bed and asleep.

How long a time had elapsed, Ryan had no
idea, but he was suddenly aroused from
slumber by the splintering of glass and the
crashing of woodwork. He sprang from his
bed, and hastily throwing on a few things,
snatched up an old double-barrelled gun
from a corner of the room, and exclaim-
ing: "There's somebody broken into the
house, Mary!" rushed down the stairs. As he
entered the kitchen, he was confronted by
seven or eight men with black crape over
their faces, armed with guns and sticks.

Ryan took in the situation at a glance. He
saw that he was "visited." Quick as thought
he threw his gun to his shoulder; but
prompt though he was, his assailants were
prompter still, and before he could pull the

trigger one of them had fired, and a heavy charge of shot struck him in the leg, and stretched him on the ground, whilst a voice exclaimed: "Take that as a receipt for your rint, you ould villain!"

At the report of the gun, Mary Ryan dashed down the stairs to her husband's assistance. As she entered the room, she stumbled over her husband's prostrate form, just as a voice called out, "Finish him!"

Two or three shots were immediately fired at the wounded man. A sharp cry escaped Mary Ryan, and she screamed out:

"You've murthered him, ye villains."

Her mother's cry and the shots brought Norah flying down the staircase. As she stood aghast in the doorway, half blind with the smoke, the apparent leader of the band exclaimed: "Best to finish the whole accursed brood," and levelled his gun at her. As he did so, one of his companions struck it up and cried:

"Damn it all! lave the colleen alone!"
There was a slight struggle between the two
men, during which the crape fell from the
face of the man who wanted to shoot her,
and Norah recognized Cassidy. Thinking her
hour was come, she covered her face with
her hands, and prepared to meet her doom.
Another second and the gun was fired, the
charge burying itself innocuously in the roof
of the cabin. Still the girl stood, her face
buried in her hands, expecting every moment
to be her last. Minutes passed, and at last
Norah ventured to raise her head and steal a
look around. The intruders had disappeared,
whilst at her feet lay the motionless forms of
her father and mother.

Norah sank upon the ground by their side,
and, slight experience as she had of death,
knew that payment of rent would never
trouble her father more, but her mother,
though wounded, was already coming to her
senses. A bitterer night in the course of her

life it may be hoped that Norah Ryan is never
destined to have than that when she watched
by the corse of her murdered father and
tended her wounded mother till the sun rose.

CHAPTER VIII.

"CASSIDY TAKES TO THE MOUNTAINS."

WHEN morning dawned, Norah felt that she must go in search of help. The girl was worn out with watching, and her nerves were shattered by the terrible scene she had gone through. Her mother, too, required the doctor's aid and, though bearing her sufferings bravely, added to her daughter's misery by her ceaseless enquiries for her husband. Why did not Timothy come to her? it was unlike him not to be by her bedside when she was ill. Ah, was he hurt, too? And poor Norah felt that she could not break to her luckless mother that Timothy Ryan would never utter word, cross or kind, to any human being again. She had composed her father's blood-stained corse and covered his face decorously with a cloth, and now she propped her mother up in bed, dressed her and told her she must leave her for a little, then wrapping her shawl around her head she sped to the parish doctor to entreat his help for her mother. Next she went to a neighbour with whom she was on intimate terms, to ask one of the girls to come over and help her in her sore need, to comfort her in her great sorrow. Molly Byrne willingly assented, and was preparing to accompany Norah when Mr. Byrne appeared upon the threshold. He listened gravely while Molly briefly narrated the particulars of the tragedy of the previous night, as she had just gathered them from Norah, and then in a somewhat husky voice and with a shamefaced expression he said :

"Take off your shawl, girl; I'll not have you mixed up in this business. Norah Ryan, no one can be more sorry for you than I am. Me heart just bleeds for your throuble. Your

father, poor fellow, rest his sowl," and here
Mr. Byrne crossed himself, "was as straight a
man over a deal or a tumbler as anny in the
barony, but I dursn't let Molly go with you.
You understand?"

But she did not. She stood like one dazed
—how could anyone refuse her help in such
sore trouble as hers? A low cry from Molly
as she burst into tears first brought the
terrible fact home to her—that fact which
Mr. Byrne had recognised as soon as he had
heard her story—that she was proscribed, that
the National League had exercised that power
of excommunication which even the Popes
have renounced for the last century and which
is solemnly *denounced* as inhuman, un-Christian-
like and unjustifiable, by the present occupant
of the chair of St. Peter. The cruellest
weapon of the Middle Ages has been repro-
duced in the nineteenth century; so much for
the progress of civilization!

Molly pressed her hand, but Norah snatched

it impatiently away. Shrouding her head in her shawl, she uttered no word, but passed out and went home to her dead—dead whom no man might bury. There the poor girl fairly broke down, and as she crouched by her dead father's side her passionate sobs fairly drowned the low wailing of her mother. The doctor; oh, yes, she could depend upon him. Dr. Connolly had put his foot down firmly from the first, and announced that he should give his services whenever they were required, whether those who called to him for aid were *excommunicated* or not. He would chance his life —a doctor was continually doing that—but should the League make his residence in the barony impossible, he would go. He could get on much better without the people than they could without him.

But, bar the doctor, who dared come to her help? She had to nurse one parent and bury the other as best she might, and a shiver ran through the girl's frame and she once more

bowed her head, as she felt that her trouble
was greater than she could bear. Suddenly
there was a noise of wheels in the lane outside. "The doether!" she ·murmured, and
rose to open the door for him.

"Oh, my poor darling!" exclaimed Katie
Eyre, as she caught her foster sister in her
arms, and kissed her passionately. "We
have just heard at the Castle of—of—what's
happened. The cowards! I never saw papa
mad with anger before; he swears he'll never
rest till he's brought the murderers to justice.
Oh! Norah, Norah"—and here Miss Eyre
fairly broke down and mingled her tears with
the fatherless girl's.

"Now," she continued, after indulging in a
good cry, "I have brought the waggonette
up, and papa says that you and your mother
are to come down to the Castle. No one," she
added, dropping her voice, "will dare help
you here."

"No," rejoined Norah, sadly; "I asked

Molly Byrne to come and stay with me a bit, but her father wouldn't let her. He said he dursn't."

" This self-constituted *Vehmgericht* is shameful," cried Kate.

Miss Eyre was well read in Scott's novels, and reminiscences of Anne of Gierstein flashed across her mind.

" I passed Doctor Connolly on my way up," she continued. " He told me your mother was wounded, too, and that we were to wait till he had been here ; and papa, too, said he should be up in the course of the morning, but he had got one or two things to see to first. I think," she added, softly, " it was something about your father's death."

Here their conversation was interrupted by the arrival of the doctor, who, after an examination of Mrs. Ryan, briefly pointed out to Miss Eyre that the carrying off of the wounded woman and Norah to the Castle was impracticable! First of all, it would not be prudent to move Mrs. Ryan for two or three days! "And besides," continued the doctor, "there must be a coroner's inquest, and poor Ryan cannot be left unwatched."

Both girls at once saw that the doctor's reasons were unanswerable, and it was settled accordingly that Mrs. Ryan and Norah should remain in their own home till after the funeral. The doctor still lingered, and the reason why he did so soon became apparent. Ratcliffe Eyre, accompanied by a magistrate and a posse of policemen, soon arrived on the scene. It was speedily settled that the cottage should be put under the protection of the police, and that a coroner's inquest should be held on the body of Timothy Ryan the next day.

"I'm going to ask you one question, Norah," said Ratcliffe Eyre, "and don't answer it unless you like. Did you recognise any of your father's murderers, and if so will you give evidence against them?"

"I recognised one," replied Norah, firmly,

25*

"and I'll swear against him before any court of justice in the counthry."

When Norah gave her evidence the next day she swore unhesitatingly that Michael Cassidy fired the shot that killed her father. She had known him for years! The crape dropped from his face and she saw him distinctly, and the result was a verdict of wilful murder against Michael Cassidy and others unknown.

Cassidy's cabin had been closely watched by the police from the hour they heard of the crime. He was known as a notorious leader of the National League, and was suspected of being concerned in more than one of the local outrages which had been perpetrated. But it was useless; it was the first time Cassidy had been actually concerned in a murder, and he had a wholesome dread of the consequences. He had not gone home after the crime, but had betaken himself with all haste to the mountains; and it was well for him that he had done so, for Ratcliffe Eyre had sworn to hang him as high as Haman, and was relentless as a sleuth-hound on his trail, but when a man reaches the Alsatia of the mountains in that country, especially when covered by the ægis of the League, it is hard to lay him by the heels, be his hands steeped never so deep in blood.

The depths of Ratcliffe Eyre's nature were stirred to their utmost by Ryan's murder. The Master of Rathkelly had been a listless man since his wife's death, but recent events had roused him from his apathy. Above all did he resent the interference of this American-nominated crew, who call themselves the representatives of the Irish Nation, and whose power was sustained by murder, mutilation, and proscription. Ryan had been an old and favourite tenant, and as we know, through his wife having nursed Miss Katie, the bonds had been further strengthened between the family and the Castle.

Eyre was of the kind that, under such circumstances, don't waste time grieving over the dead. He had vowed to avenge the death of his tenant, and with all the tenacity of his nature he hounded on the police to arrest the fugitive whom the dead man's daughter had solemnly sworn was her father's assassin. Pressed for money too, as he was, he was lavish of it in this cause; and so fiercely was the hunt conducted, that again and again Cassidy escaped the clutches of the police, or Ratcliffe Eyre and his myrmidons, by a bare half-hour. But if the desire for vengeance was unslaked in one man, a dogged spirit of savage resentment was aroused in the other.

If Eyre thirsted to bring Cassidy to account for his crime, Cassidy on the other hand hungered for vengeance on the Master of Rathkelly, and to settle matters with Terence Flynn.

The League were much struck with the

impression that their first blow had produced, and were resolved to supplement it as speedily as possible with a second, which they concluded would place the whole district prostrate at their feet. That Cassidy was in constant communication with the local branch of the League, need scarcely be said. A man like him, placed without the pale, and with a verdict of wilful murder recorded against him, was an emissary they were only too glad to have at their disposal ; and Mike Cassidy fiercely argued, that if it had been necessary to make an example of Ryan for paying his rent, it was no less necessary to do so with Terence Flynn. True, they had not the direct proof against him that they had had against Ryan, but there could be no moral doubt but that he was a like offender. "And," continued Mike, in his argument, "if the League is to live, it must make its *ordthers* respected."

There were those present at the meeting

who, though they did not venture to say so,
thought that the counsel of a man with a
rope round his neck should be taken with
some misgiving. But, flushed with the
success of their first great outrage, McDermot
and the majority of the local council agreed
that a second blow could not be struck too
soon, and, yielding to the arguments of the
blood-stained Cassidy, it was determined that
Terence Flynn should follow poor Ryan to
the land of shades.

By this time Norah and her mother had
been moved down to the Castle. The cabin
was locked up, and the farm—one of the best
on the estate—stood untenanted. Mrs. Ryan
was too ill to manage it, even if she had been
competent ; but she wished to resign it,
though both she and her landlord well knew
that no man on the country side would dare
offer himself as a tenant. Eyre, too, could
not help noticing that his tenantry looked
askance at him whenever he came across

them. It was not the look of sullen dislike and hatred, it was the furtive look of men who dared no longer acknowledge him. Eyre was far too shrewd a man not to understand this.

"Not boycotted yet," he muttered to himself, "but on the verge of it."

The Master of Rathkelly was right. If he had not as yet been proscribed, his case had been taken into consideration. He was one of the landlords whom the League most detested in that locality, on account of his haughty defiance of their authority. He was now adding to his misdemeanours by sheltering the wife and daughter of their latest victim, and by the strenuous efforts he was making to apprehend the murderer. It went for nothing in his behalf that Mrs. Ryan and Norah were two helpless women, to whom no one else dared offer help in their hour of need. Nor was it to be taken into consideration that, as an active magistrate, Ratcliffe Eyre was doing no more than his duty in endeavouring to apprehend a criminal who richly deserved to expiate his offending. McDermot and his friends marked the relentless pertinacity with which Eyre pursued his quarry, and it somewhat perturbed them. Such an active upholder of the law would interfere not a little with their schemes. The apostles of anarchy and disorder stood some chance of seeing their followers cowed by the upholding of the statute book, and that infringement of the sixth commandment should be speedily followed by the dispensation of the stern old Mosaic law—"An eye for an eye," "A tooth for a tooth," "A life for a life," a doctrine extremely inconvenient to the professors of assassination.

It need hardly be said that no threats or fear of the League kept Terence from constantly going down to Rathkelly, and Norah clung to him in her sorrow, and leant on him

more than she had ever done in the days
before her father's death. All the girl's
coquettish ways had vanished, and her pale
sad face looked fondly up at her lover in a
manner that made Terence's heart ache.
The young man's very nature seemed changed;
he had been excessively shocked at the brutal
murder of Ryan, and was perfectly aware that
his own turn might come next. His mother,
too, was ailing, and the Ryan tragedy had
been a tremendous shock to her. They had
been close neighbours and intimate friends
from the day Timothy Ryan brought his bride,
then a slip of a colleen, home. Terence felt
that he now held his home on a most precarious tenure, not from any difference with
his landlord, but on account of this unlicensed
body who had taken on themselves to arbi-
trate between the owners of land and their
tenants. If they would only leave him in peace
during his mother's life-time—she was a
weak old woman now and her days in the

world were not likely to be of long duration
—he would be content. He would make
a home for himself in some other country
where the League should cease from troubling
and workers were at peace.

"No, Terence," his sweetheart would say,
"I am yours whenever you can claim me. I
won't marry you now ; if I did I should
only bring the Moonlighters upon you. I
should, perhaps, see you dead at my feet,
unless in their mercy they killed me too.
We must wait for betther times, darlint."

Terence Flynn kissed and comforted the
girl. In good truth, he knew Norah was far
safer under Ratcliffe Eyre's roof than she
could be under his own, and that the girl
had identified the assassin of her father, and
was prepared to give evidence against him,
was now known all through the country.

CHAPTER IX.

"PROSCRIBED IN THE HOUSE OF GOD."

It is a big night at Westminster. Government is intent on passing what their opponents stigmatize as a Coercion Act, but which, in the eyes of all logical, thinking men, is simply an act to compel the better observance of law and order in Ireland. Honorable members for Ireland dissent in a manner which, to paraphrase Wordsworth, is as "four score groaning like one." Eminent Orator, more firmly possessed than ever with the idea that the salvation of the kingdom depends on his shortly being restored to power, and utterly oblivious of the repressive measures he took under similar circumstances some few

years ago, thunders forth, " We do not now, as
in the days described by Lord Cornwallis,
employ torture and murder as instruments of
Irish Government."

Flippant junior ornament to the Treasury
Bench springs to his feet, and jerks in the
observation: " Quite so, but the National
League do." Eminent Orator rising in his
wrath, proceeds to administer a severe castiga-
tion to his juvenile commentator, which only
produces a titter from the culprit's friends,
and a whispered observation that " Dandy
Church had drawn the old 'un again!"

That Messrs. Last, Carmody, and other Irish
patriots, had much to say on the subject, it
is needless to mention, though the pacification
of Ireland, perhaps, was not exactly the thing
these gentlemen wanted. The tranquillizing
of Ireland meant the collapse of the National
League, and, to men like Last and Carmody,
this meant the doing away with their business.
Politics is a game which requires a cool head,

but though the chiefs may play as calmly as
if they were at the chess table, yet they are
compelled to trust in a great measure to their
subordinates, and the chiefs of the Irish
Brigade must have more than once cursed the
excessive zeal of their too zealous supporters.

Eminent Orator having confided to the
House that his utterances of three or four
years ago had been altogether mi-understood ;
and having, after an eloquent speech of an
hour and forty-five minutes, left his hearers
still more fogged than before as to what
might be his sentiments on the Irish, or
indeed, any other question, sat down amidst
tumultuous cheering. His auditors clear on
one point only, to wit, that he was quite ready
to assume office again whenever he could
manage to oust the occupants of the Treasury
Bench from their present position. Mr.
Last distinguished himself by a speech which
for fatuous iteration surpassed everything he
had yet achieved, while Dan Carmody exhibited

a command of vituperation exceeding all yet known at St. Stephen's, and after having been called to order some half-dozen times, finally attained the distinction of being suspended for a month.

Party feeling runs high. Nobody concerns themselves much about the violent diatribes of the Irish Press, but the Radical papers rave about the shameful interference with "the liberties of the subject"—good stock phrase, which has done duty now for some centuries. Flippant junior ornament of Treasury Bench suggests in smoking-room that the Rads have not quite mastered the phrase, the bill is to suppress "the liberties *taken* by the subject," that murder, as the bard of the Ingoldsbys puts it, is "coming it strong," and the awful tragedy of the Ryans is a charge which the Irish Brigade find easier to disown than to extenuate. But even the efforts of the paid patriots of Hibernia could do no more than delay the bill. Its passing

was inevitable, and passed it accordingly was
by what the Radical prints pleasantly stigma-
tized as a brutal Conservative majority. And
then the prophets went out into the byeways
and prophesied that Home Rule could not be
long delayed—prophesying after the manner
of their race that which they wished to come
to pass. The prophets of Ireland were perhaps
an exception to this rule, neither wishing nor
expecting that this dubious boon should be
bestowed upon their country.

When the news came across St. George's
Channel that the Crimes Act was passed,
Messrs McDermot, Cassidy and Co., although
slightly disconcerted, were by no means
seriously so. They had seen this sort of thing
before. The law of the English parliament,
after having been enforced in half-hearted
fashion for a year or two, had been usually done
away with by the new Government that had
superseded the old, and things went on once
more in the old fashion, and the National

League once more ruled over all Ireland, with
the exception of Ulster. Messrs McDermot,
Cassidy and Co., their heads a little turned
by the terror they had caused in the district,
and the almost complete rule they had
obtained over the entire community, meditated
deeply on striking one more blow to con-
solidate their dominion. That Cassidy should
take this line was but natural. He had
denounced Terence Flynn, and to do away
with him and, if possible, with Norah Ryan and
the Master of Rathkelly, would gratify not
only his private hatred but, as he believed, do
away with all witnesses of his crimes.

Messrs Carmody and Last are rather aghast
at the promptitude with which their followers
have responded to their inflammatory
harangues. The word has been passed
through the Irish ranks that it is inexpedient
for the present to excite the people, that for
the present all outrage is to be discouraged,
and Moonlighters are at a discount. It is

easy to fire the prairie, but what man can arrest the flames? Kindle the passions of the people, and don't be surprised if they are speedily out of your hand! Messrs. Last and Carmody had set a conflagration going round Callowtown which they were now powerless to restrain. Crafty McDermot found in it the indulgence of two passions apt to be dear to most men, power and the greed of gold, for a fair sprinkling of money from America passed through those close-clutching fingers of his, and neither he nor the fugitive Cassidy were inclined to stop in their career of intimidation. A reign of terror must be always progressive! Let those who groan under it once cease to fear, and the tyranny is dead.

Norah Ryan, so far, has hardly set foot outside the gates of Rathkelly Castle. The Police Officer has frankly told her that her life is no longer safe; and insists upon it that, when she wishes to go outside its gates, she should do so under a police

escort. He further counsels Mr. Eyre to put
himself under similar protection; but the
stern Master of Rathkelly replied fiercely
that there never was an Eyre yet whose
hand couldn't keep his head, and that if the
Moonlighters paid him a visit it would probably be " bad " for the Moonlighters! The
officer could only shake his head, for he
knew well that Ratcliffe Eyre was a marked
man by the League; and that the strenuous
attempts that he not only had made, but was
yet making, to apprehend the assassin,
Cassidy, had still further inflamed them
against him.

One thing that Norah was very anxious
about was to attend mass. She longed to
ask comfort from her Maker, and to make
arrangements with the priest that sundry
masses should be said for the soul of her
murdered father. She was dreadfully nervous
about this, her first appearance in public.
She could not forget her great friend, Molly

Byrne, had not been allowed to come to her in her trouble. Surely her neighbours would show some sympathy for a girl left fatherless under such terrible circumstances. How if they all shrank from her? She wondered how she should bear it, if they did. She confided her fears to her young mistress, and high-spirited Katie at once exclaimed:

"They can never be such cowards, Norah! though that terror of the League is a thing one never could have believed in if one had not seen it! I will go with you. I am not of your faith—but that does not matter— there can be no reason why I shouldn't sit beside you."

So when Sunday came, the two girls started—under police escort—for the chapel, which stood about a mile from Rathkelly. They arrived there in good time, and seated themselves quietly in by no means promi- nent places. Gradually the building began to fill, and Norah, whose head was bent, and

her face buried in her hands, was not at first
recognized by the congregation ; but Miss
Eyre's face was fully exposed, and, of course,
perfectly well known to everyone in the
chapel. It naturally attracted attention to
her companion, and soon it was whispered
around that Norah Ryan was in their midst!
A hurried consultation took place, and then
the men, with one accord, rose and walked
silently out of the chapel. Norah cowered
on her knees, but not so Miss Eyre! She
rose to her feet, and, with flushed face, and
her little head thrown well back, looked
defiantly at the men as they filed past her.
To do them justice, not one dared meet the
dark blue eyes that flashed with such ineffable
scorn. Hardly had the men disappeared,
when an ominous flutter was seen amongst
the women. Another two minutes, and they
had followed the example of their lords and
masters ; and the officiating priest, with the
two girls, were left the sole tenants of the

building. Norah's prayers were soon said, and her interview with the priest was soon over. As soon as they were outside the chapel, Miss Eyre's wrath found vent, and in no measured terms did she denounce the cowardly agitators who were ruining her country.

"Ah! what have I done?" said Norah, sobbing; "they have killed my father, and now they have cast me out from among them as if I was a leper, and only because I tould it was Cassidy done it. What girl could do otherwise?"

"Hush! Norah," said Miss Eyre. "It's horrible to think that men can treat a woman in such a manner! The head of your Church pronounces it unjustifiable before God, and I think that I have heard that the great Austrian general who treated the Hungarian women in some such fashion was well hooted by the crowd when he came to London."

Norah walked on in silence; the girl was

perfectly dazed by the position in which she
found herself. Her father dead! her home
broken up! the cattle all maimed and muti-
lated, and herself a pariah in her own little
world! She could not understand it; *what*
had brought all these horrors on her head?
As far as she could make out, her poor
father's sole offence had been the paying
what he owed. Norah had been brought up
with a somewhat indistinct idea that there
were divers pains and penalties incumbent on
those who did *not* pay their debts. And the
policy of the Land League puzzled her poor
little brains as it did those of many others.

Ratcliffe Eyre was furious when he heard
the shameful story of that morning. " They
may beat me," he said ; " they have alienated
my tenants! they have boycotted my hounds!
they have attempted—ah! never mind that!
—but, by the Living God, I'll never bow
my neck to the orders of the League!
Whatever happens, I'll play the game out,

and, if it comes to the worst, I'll look for a home on the other side of St. George's Channel."

From this out there was no disguise about the enmity between Ratcliffe Eyre and the League. Although he still scorned the aid of the police, the bolts, bars, and fastenings of the house were jealously looked to every evening. Greatly as the establishment had been reduced, yet the two or three old servitors who were left were men he could thoroughly rely on. The old butler, who had been in his service from his youth and who had periodically given warning during the last twenty years, could not possibly have pictured to himself any other place than that he held at Rathkelly Castle, and to do him justice, though his wages were more irregularly paid than they had ever been before, he never even hinted at leaving the service of his life-time. Poor O'Reilly had partially recovered from the skirmish at Ballater Gorse,

and though his vocation was gone, still hung
about the place, looking after the two or
three horses that yet remained, and doing
any odd jobs that might come to his hand.
Mr. Eyre had lately insisted on his sleeping
in the house. Both he and the butler were
old men, but they understood how to handle
firearms, and both guns and pistols were
plentiful at Rathkelly. The garrison indeed
was stronger than the outside world gave
it credit for ; O'Reilly, though an elderly
man could shoot, and veterans of the Old
Guard had before now proved themselves
more than a match for the wild onslaught of
the conscripts. One more auxiliary might
perhaps be counted. Miss Katie, amongst her
many unfeminine accomplishments, reckoned
considerably dexterity in the use of both
pistol and shot-gun, and with her daring
temper might prove a very useful recruit
should the Castle be laid siege to in earnest.
As for the Master, there was never a man in

the barony but would shrink from meeting him face to face. Although getting on in years, his fierce, ruthless temper and excellence in all manner of field sports, whether with horse, rod, or gun, was a tradition in the country, and nobody doubted that the man who in fair fight attempted Ratcliffe Eyre's life carried his own in his hand.

The route had come at last, and the —th had received orders to proceed to Cork, and thence embark for Bristol, Aldershot being their final destination. The distracted state of the country made no difference to this arrangement, as the place of the —th was at once taken by another of Her Majesty's regiments. Such officers as had been on visiting terms with the Rathkelly people hastened to pay their farewell visits, but none had been so intimate at the Castle as Sturton and Tom Chester, and these two drove over somewhat sadly to make their adieux.

"It's not leaving the country, Tom, one

feels sorry for. In the old days, for a sports-
man one could ask no better quarters; but,
as we've seen, that's all over now. But I'm
real sorry for those we are going to say good-
bye to. Eyre's a marked man, and must be
a well-nigh ruined one to boot; and it's hard
lines on that girl."

"I'd take care of her fast enough, if she
would only give me the right," rejoined
young Chester.

"Don't despair, Tom. She's young, and
don't know what she likes, as yet."

"She knows what she doesn't, though,"
replied the other moodily; "and the minute
I try to speak seriously to her she laughs it
off, and evades coming to the point."

"Well, you'll have a chance to-day," rejoined Sturton. "The Master is certain to
go in for a talk with me, and that will leave
you a clear field with the young lady." And
here they pulled up at the gates of Rathkelly.

CHAPTER X.

The —th have arrived at the permanent
barracks at Aldershot, and ere Sturton has
been a couple of days in the camp, he is
apprised that Colonel Belton's regiment of
Hussars has been telegraphed as on its way
up Channel, and may be hourly expected.
He wonders what the Beltons will do. Will
Mrs. Belton join her husband, or will she
continue to keep on that house in London?
Although his feelings for Grace can hardly
be yet said to be extinguished, he is quite
aware that it is utterly dead on her side: that
she likes him as an old friend, but nothing
more. Still, he thinks if the Beltons set up
their ménage there, it will make that great

dust-ridden camp considerably more endurable. Being an enthusiastic soldier is one
thing, but it is quite compatible with a desire
that your surroundings, when off duty, should
be pleasant. Aldershot, though healthy, is
rather trying in one respect, the weather
never quite suits it; either the plague of dust
or mud predominates.

But Sturton was not left long in doubt on
that point; no sooner had the —th Hussars
marched into camp than he left his card on
their mess, and called pointedly on their
Colonel. As an old friend of his wife and
her family, Belton received him cordially,
and told him that Grace would join him there
as soon as he had got a house ready for her.
"As for the youngsters, he added, "it's just
time they went to a small school of some
sort. I don't hold with rearing boys at home,
they grow up soft. Times are pretty bad, I
fancy, all around Rathkelly?"

"I should say they couldn't be worse,"

rejoined Sturton, " only I feel sure they will be. Thanks to the League, all reliance between man and man is destroyed, and no one would be rash enough to invest capital in a country so torn by internal dissension ; but Mrs. Belton can tell you all this better than I can. I'll say good-bye now, Colonel, for no doubt you've lots to arrange at present."

" Good-bye. Mind you come and see us when we're settled."

To this Sturton gave a hearty assent, and so the two men parted.

There was one man at Aldershot to whom the salt seemed to have lost its savour, and that was Tom Chester. He had nerved himself to have it out with Katie Eyre that last day at Rathkelly, and though she had parried the attack laughingly, as long as she could, he had compelled her to listen to him. The girl had been serious enough then, and more sweet and gentle with him than she had ever been before. But she had told him firmly, though softly, it never could be; that she had a great esteem for him, should always be proud to count him among her friends, but that she had no love to give him such as he deserved, and she hoped he might one day win——

No one who knew Katie would have given her credit for the feeling and good taste she displayed in declining her first offer.

"I have asked you too soon," said Tom, in the bitterness of his disappointment. "If I had only given you more time you might——."

"No, Mr. Chester," interrupted the girl eagerly, as her face flushed. "It would have been all the same; I could never be your wife."

"I suppose there's someone you like better," replied the young man moodily.

"Mr. Chester," cried Katie indignantly, and crimsoning up to the roots of her hair in spite of herself.

"I beg pardon," he replied, "I had no business to say that. I am afraid there's nothing more for me to say than good-bye, and wish you all happiness in the future," and he stretched forth his hand.

Miss Eyre took it in silence, but made no reply. And so finishe 1 Tom Chester's wooing at Rathkelly.

Colonel Belton lost very little time in establishing himself in a house at no great distance from the permanent barracks, where Grace at once joined him. Sturton and Tom Chester speedily became intimates of the Belton ménage, and to the latter Grace was always exceedingly gracious. She had a pretty accurate inkling of how it had fared with him at Rathkelly, and felt that he had deserved to have sped better in his love chase. "A foolish child, that sister of mine," thought Grace, judging her as the experienced matron usually does the girl who declines an advantageous settlement, quite forgetting the

time when she had her ideal of love's young
dream, and ways and means were as nothing
compared to two hearts beating in unison.
Well, that phase does not last long, and it
is as well, perhaps, for the hearts don't beat
quite so evenly when there is trouble about
meeting the weekly bills.

"I am afraid things are going from bad to
worse with papa," said Mrs. Belton to Sturton,
one afternoon, as he loitered by the side of
her tea-table.

"It's the same with the landed interest
everywhere. Here, they endeavour to make
the best of it; in Ireland, they make the
worst of it. This incessant agitation does
no good."

"No. My poor Aunt Jemima—such a
handsome old woman she is, papa used always
to say none of us girls were in it with Aunt
Jim—she had a nice little income for a
spinster, but she's had to give up her house,
sell her furniture, and take refuge in a second

rate London boarding-house. Hard lines at
her age, and no assurance that her income
won't vanish altogether."

Sturton made no reply. He had no comfort to suggest, and thought indeed that
nothing was more likely to happen than that
Miss Jemima should find the humble pittance
she counted on had disappeared.

"How does Katie bear up against all this
trouble?" continued Mrs. Belton. "She
must find life getting somewhat sad at
Rathkelly."

"She's astonished me by the way she
faces it. I regarded her till quite lately as
a rather precocious child, but circumstances
seem to have made her a woman all at
once."

"Yes," said Mrs. Belton musingly, "I can
fancy that. It often is so. Some of our
most butterfly officers in India turned out
veritable paladins when the tug came. Never
believe your dandies can't fight, or that your

girls have not a dash of the Maid of Sara-
gossa in them when tried."

"No," replied Sturton. "I've gone through
my baptism of fire, and seen a young one,
who was almost the butt of the regiment,
lead on his men through a '*feu d'enfer*' as
recklessly as any Bayard could have done."

"Mr. Chester was very sweet on her, was
he not?"

"You can't expect me to tell secrets out
of school," rejoined Sturton laughing.

"No reason you should," said Mrs. Belton.
"I know he was. Pity she couldn't fancy
him. He was a good match for her."

"Plenty of time to set that right," replied
Sturton. "If Tom is in earnest, he won't
take a girl's first rebuff for an answer."

"He'll get none other," said Grace. "I'm
sorry for it, but she'll never marry Mr.
Chester; good thing, though, it would be
for her."

"Why not?"

"Oh! I can't say. *We* know these things intuitively. You men are so stupid."

"Perhaps so," returned Sturton, as he rose to take leave. "I can only retort that your sex are so incomprehensible, which is a confession of ignorance about the most interesting study of *our* lives."

"Very prettily put. Good-bye, Captain Sturton. Mind you come again before long. George wants to see you about a bit of riding. You mayn't understand us, but when you've to reckon with your fellows in a race you certainly require no prompting."

"What is it?" enquired Sturton briefly.

"You must see him, but I think he wants you to ride something for him in the Grand Military. The two or three we have in the regiment, that are fair horsemen, are engaged on their own account, and George is a good stone too heavy. Come in and see him about it."

"Certainly. If he can't do better I'll be his substitute with pleasure."

"Do better," laughed Mrs. Belton. "No affectation of modesty, sir. You won for Katie, mind you do as much for me."

Mrs. Belton saw no more of Sturton for two or three days, and was just beginning to wonder what had become of him, when the truant made his appearance.

"I have run in to say good-bye," he exclaimed. "I am off this evening. General Carnegie, who was my first chief, has just got the Western command, and he has offered to take me on his staff."

"We shall be sorry to lose you, but I suppose it is a good thing for you," rejoined Mrs. Belton.

"Yes," he replied. "Next to being on active service, one's best chance of getting on nowadays is staff work of some sort."

"I suppose so," she said, musingly, "but you must see George before you go. I think

I heard him come in just now," and so saying
Mrs. Belton touched the bell, and told the
servant to let his master know Captain
Sturton was in the drawing-room.

The colonel entered the room in a few
minutes. A tall, fine-looking man, the *beau
ideal* of a dragoon if somewhat tall for an
hussar. He congratulated Sturton as they
shook hands, saying : " I heard of it at the
Adjutant-General's office. Nice thing for
you, and Carnegie, as you know, is a
right good fellow. Grace told you I'd a
favour to ask of you—that I want you to
ride for me in the Grand Military next
spring? "

" Yes, and I told Mrs. Belton I would. I
shall have no trouble with Carnegie about a
week's leave for the 'Soldiers' races,' I'm
sure."

" It's very good of you. The horse should
have a very decent chance, but I was at my
wit's end for a jock. I've been in India so

long I've rather lost touch of the gentlemen riders."

"Never fear. Captain Sturton won't fail us," said Mrs. Belton, gaily.

"No; but even if I did you know how to replace me."

"Indeed, I do not," rejoined Grace.

"Yes, if anything unforeseen should prevent my riding, ask Tom Chester."

"Mr. Chester!"

"Yes, you saw him ride his first steeple-chase, Mrs. Belton. He was riding an awkward horse, only just schooled to a bank country, and the pair ran green. Still he rode that race right well till he fell into the usual novice's error, he was a little too eager to get home; he'll do better next time."

"Yes," said Grace, "I recollect it very well, and there was a moment when papa thought Loadstone would win."

"Just so," replied Sturton, laughing, "and the time's not far off when they will not only

cry 'Chester wins,' but he will win. In racing
slang, Mrs. Belton, 'Never let him run
loose.'"

"That means always back him for a little,"
rejoined Mrs. Belton.

"Exactly. The colonel knows what I
mean. And now good-bye to both of you,"
and with a cordial pressure of the hands
Sturton took his departure.

That Mrs. Belton in her letters home should
mention that the —th were quartered at
Aldershot, and that she saw a good deal of
Sturton and Chester, was but natural. Katie
in her now lonely life received this intelligence
with morbid jealousy.

"Does she want them all?" she murmured,
angrily, perfectly regardless of the fact that
one of them, at all events, she had herself
rejected. "It's too bad of Grace. She's
married herself, and I'm sure it's bad form to
keep a lot of men dangling about her."

Katie Eyre had set her passionate little

heart on one man, and it was gall and ver-
juice to her to think that this man apparently
preferred her married sister to herself. There
had been no doubt about it ; while the —th
had been quartered at Conroy, Sturton had
taken much more pleasure in Mrs. Belton's
society than in her own. He had been
courteous enough, but the amused smile
which had occasionally played about his lips
at her petulance had irritated her to madness.
He *would* regard her as a child, and Katie,
somewhat precocious for her years, felt that,
whatever she might look, she had become a
woman. Girls of her age can be very much
in earnest in their first love-dream, and that
the object of their worship should fail to
recognize the prize he has won naturally
exasperates them. " Were it not for Grace,"
Kate argued, " Captain Sturton would have
been at my feet long ago. As it was he
could not forget that old affair of years gone
by, and it was scandalous," she said passion-

ately to herself, "that Mrs. Belton should strive to keep alive that old attachment."

Miss Eyre was, as we know, by no means accurate in her deductions; we are not wont to be at seventeen; and when our love affairs at that age do not run smooth, which they rarely do, are wont to rail bitterly against those either real or imaginary, whom we conceive to have interfered with them. We fall in love in those days usually with the ideal, we drape our idol in robes of our own weaving, and rage to find it insensible to the incense we burn before it. Later on we have learnt better, and expect, at all events, more or less reciprocity from the outset. Life, as Mrs. Belton justly surmised, was very dull for Katie just now, and the girl had little to do but to grind her white teeth and fume, after the manner of most disappointed young women.

Times indeed were going very hard with the district all round Callowtown. The iron yoke of the League was upon them, and they were groaning under a despotism such as had not been known in the United Kingdom during the century. Good old tenants who had been on friendly terms with their landlords, such as those on the Rathkelly barony, were beginning to murmur. Their landlords had endeavoured to meet the bad times by a deduction of thirty or more per cent. in their rents, and they had been seduced into rebellion against their old masters by the promise of holding their farms rent-free. If they were to pay this assessed rent to the League, as more than one of them grumbled, " I'd as soon pay it to ould Eyre himself ; he was a good sort, annyway ! and at all events, if we paid him we ran no risk of eviction ! it's little McDermot could do for us if that came about, nor that Last and Dan Carmody either." They might get drunk with enthusiasm at the fervid harangues of their leaders, but the farmers generally had no very great respect for them, they were beginning to recognize that this political dream, although a very comfortable thing for those—well, let us say engaged in promoting it—should it be carried out, would make their labourers their masters. Communism, or the redistribution of property, is always in favour of the gentleman who has least. The Crimes Act had passed, and the question was whether the Government would dare to make use of it now they had obtained the power. Blustering subordinates like McDermot, trembling for their pocket-money, argued that it should be met by a strong counter demonstration on the part of "a down-throdden" nationality. And though their more astute leaders might counsel prudence privately, yet most assuredly their public harangues were not calculated to impress it.

As the old French defender of capital punishment said, it was " messieurs les assassins!" who commenced! And it was

getting high time that the moonlight murderer should be emphatically convinced that
the rope awaited him if convicted, and that
mutilation, boycotting, and such crimes would
also be taken prompt cognizance of by the
law. And as these manifold offences meet
their deserts once more arises that well-worn
national cry of " Justice for Oireland !"

CHAPTER XI.

" BY HIS MOTHER'S DEATH BED."

RATCLIFFE EYRE continues his search for
Cassidy with untiring perseverance, and as
Jack Blake said to his wife, "if the bringing of Moonlighters to justice were always
carried out with the persistence Eyre has
brought to the task, faith they would find
murder too dangerous an amusement to
indulge in." There was a heavy reward,
offered by Government, for Mike's appre-
hension, which, combined with the unflagging
raids of the police amongst the mountains,
made the criminal's position almost un-
endurable; again and again he had got
notice of the approach of his pursuers, only
just in time to escape falling into the toils

—still whisky was plenty in the Galtees and though hard hunted Cassidy was like a wolf at bay yearning only to rend the hunters before he died—if die he must. That the Nationalists should endeavour to make capital even out of this was only to be expected. McDermot and others exclaimed loudly against the brutal tyranny of the Master of Rathkelly in "hounding a man to his doom." Good stock property expression of Dan Carmody's this, which had been appropriated by his admirers.

The consequence of all these rides through the mountains in pursuit of the murderer, was that Ratcliffe Eyre got to know the police much more intimately than he had done previously; the officer especially was a very smart officer and an intelligent man.

"Mr. Eyre," he said one day as they were riding home, after another unsuccessful raid in the Galtees. "You really ought not to move about without an escort. We know

a good deal we don't talk of, and though
I can't say that any attack has been
actually planned upon you, yet, I do know
that you're a marked man and that your
life may be attempted any time."

"Thank you, Collins," was the stern reply,
"I carry my escort here," and Ratcliffe Eyre
just touched his breast pocket.

"May I ask if you were ever shot at?"
asked the officer, and he looked keenly at
his companion as he put the question.

"Why do you ask?" rejoined the other.

"I'll tell you," replied the officer.
"When you were brought before the bench
at Callowtown, about that business of McDermot's, it came to my knowledge, from a source
that I could depend upon, that this man
Cassidy had bragged in his cups, the night
before, that you shouldn't sleep in Rathkelly
on the morrow, that if the magistrates didn't
prevent you, he would, that it would be lucky
for you if you were put in prison, and a deal

more brag of that sort. I knew his lease was
out and that you had given him due notice
that you wouldn't renew. Putting this and
that together, I honestly thought that your
life was in danger that afternoon, and I
ordered a couple of my men to follow you
pretty closely. However, you slipped away
so quickly that you got much more start
than we intended. However, for all that, I
don't suppose you were ever more than a
quarter of a mile in front of them. Just
before they came to Stapleton's plantation
they heard a shot, and at once pushed rapidly
forward. They saw nothing of you, but
shortly after passing the plantation met
Terence Flynn, who told them you had just
passed, riding quickly. They continued to
follow you till they came to the gates of
Rathkelly, and then, as they could see
nothing of you, rode quietly away. I saw
Flynn myself some days afterwards; like my
men, he had heard the shot, but knew

nothing more, and we both kept our thoughts to ourselves. There are only two men who really know the story of that shot Mr. Eyre, that's yourself and the man who fired it."

Ratcliffe Eyre listened attentively to the officer's story. Yes, he recollected that shot, and had never doubted whose was the finger that pulled the trigger; but he made no reply to his companion's question, and though the latter scanned his features narrowly, he could make nothing out of Eyre's stern impassable face. Once more the officer urged the advisability of Mr. Eyre's putting himself under police protection.

"You see, sir, when they've once committed murder—have taken to the mountains and are hard hunted—they are apt to get tigerish like. This fellow, Cassidy's, chief diversion now consists in attending secret meetings of the League, where he is made a

28*

bit of a hero of, and listens to the most inflammatory harangues. It's my impression that
when a man has once committed a cold-
blooded murder of this kind he don't stick
very much at a second. I fancy Cassidy will
give more trouble yet before we catch him."

However, once more the owner of Rathkelly
declined police protection, and with a friendly
nod to the officer and his men, turned off
on his homeward way.

Mr. McDermot, in the meantime, was more
determined than ever that it was expedient
another blow should be struck. It had been
determined to do so, and what good was there
in delaying. Wasn't Mike Cassidy just the
boy for the job, and wouldn't he lead them as
he had done before. Mr. McDermot, like his
betters, was consulting his own interest in
consolidating the Reign of Terror, and had no
intention of risking his own neck in the carrying out of his schemes. He fancied a few
more midnight murders would thoroughly

cow the authorities, and could not perceive
that if the Government only resolutely carried
out the Crimes Act, the death of the League
was a mere matter of time. What he chiefly
feared was the contributions from America
falling short, and he was aware that their
supporters over there expected a show for
heir money.

"What are we waiting for?" exclaimed
the blatant orator. "Wasn't it decided that
Terry Flynn should be the next example,
and be jabers, the sooner it's done the
betther."

"Poor divil!" exclaimed another member
of the Committee, "they tell me his ould
mother is dyin'."

"An' what if she is?" replied Mr. McDermot. "Is an ould woman's life to stand
betune us and the great cause of our counthry.
No, bhoys, a few weeks can't matther to her,
and I tell ye days, nay hours, does to us. Pass
the whiskey some of yez, shure talkin's dhry

work," said the orator as he sat down, "it's doin' we ought to be."

As far as Mr. McDermot was concerned he took care to confine himself strictly to the former branch of patriotism.

The member of the Callowtown District Committee was correctly informed. Mrs. Flynn, who had long been a delicate woman, had never got over the shock she had received on hearing of the terrible fate of her old neighbour, Tim Ryan. She had taken it into her head, and not as we know without good grounds, that a similar destiny threatened her Terence. There was no doubt about it, the old lady was sinking fast, and her son knew it as well as she. The doctor had told him that morning that his mother's hours were numbered. He had loved her well, and as far as mere age went she might still have reckoned on several years yet to come, but she had been ailing a long time. A nervous anxiety lest aught should befall Terence, and

she should find herself left desolate in the
land, had worn the thread of her existence to
its thinnest.

" Thanks, Biddy, darlint," she murmured
to an old gossip who was tenderly nursing
her, " it's little more ye can do for me than
just close the eyes of me, but I'd loike just to
say good-bye to the boy. Send him to me,
alanah! and just wait in the next room while I
have a last word with him."

Terence came promptly in obedience to his
mother's summons, and sat himself down by
her bedside.

" Wisht, dear," she murmured, as she took
his strong young muscular hand between her
own thin, withered palms. " Ye must'nt grieve
for me, Terry, for I'm well out of a world
that these new men are making harder for
us day by day. Listen, darlint, to what I've
got to say to you. As soon as you have lain
me by the side of your father, promise me to
give up the place, and give up the counthry.

Your father's people, like the Ryan's there, have been in the land now many, many years, but these strangers will let you stay here no longer. You must go, Terry, dear, lest worse happens to you. There's no home for ye in the ould counthry. Promise me —— "

"I cannot lave Norah," he replied slowly.

"No," rejoined Mrs. Flynn, "I'd neither wish it nor ask it. Take her with ye, dear. I love her. I can't say more, my chest's that throublesome. Kiss me, Terry, and thin I'll thry and get a little sleep."

Terence laid his lips to his mother's pale cheek; he was conscious that the chills of death were already gathering fast around her; and soon she sank into a gentle slumber with his hand clasped in her own. Fainter and fainter grew the respiration, and more than once the young man gazed wistfully at the still face and wondered whether his mother was yet alive. At last came a faint spasm, a slight convulsive pressure of the

hand and Terence knew that his mother's
soul was sped. He called Mrs. Mahoney
and begged her to render the first sad offices
to the dead, and that done, suggested that she
had better go home while daylight lasted;
thanked her for her kindness and said he
would keep vigil over his mother's remains
that night himself.

Terence sat brooding far into the night,
and thinking over his mother's last words.
She was right, he must go; must leave the
old cabin he'd been born in, the old holding
on which he'd been reared. It was hard,
times were bad it was true, but he could
manage to get a living out of the land if he
was not interfered with. He knew too well
that what had happened to poor Ryan might
be his own lot any night. Even if Norah
would consent it would be madness to bring
her home here as his wife. He knew full
well that there was a black mark against him
in the books of the League. And as for

Norah, had she not dared to identify the murderer of her father? It was little likely that they would be left to enjoy a long lease of the old holding.

"No," he thought sadly, "there was nothing for it but to go, and after I have laid my mother in her grave as soon as I can persuade Norah to come with me I'll try my luck the other side St. George's Channel."

Suddenly a slight noise arrested his attention. It came from the room downstairs, and it flashed across him that in the first flush of the emotions caused by his loss he had taken little heed to the fastenings of door or window when he let Mrs. Mahoney out. He could hear the door open, a shuffling of footsteps, the low muttering of voices, and knew full well that the Moonlighters were upon him. Suddenly up the staircase came a gruff voice:

"Where are yez, Terence Flynn?" it asked.

"Here with my dead," was the brief rejoinder.

Once more he could hear a muffled discussion going on and then the same voice that he had heard before and which, though disguised, he recognised as Cassidy's, said in slightly raised tones:

"Go 'long with your doubts, didn't we come here to do't?"

"Terence Flynn," shouted a voice once more up the staircase. "Come down at onest, or it'll be the worst for yez."

He threw a quick glance round the room; he had no firearms or he might have held the stair. There was no weapon but an old blackthorn, once his father's. He snatched it from the wall where it hung, gripped it close and then his reply rang out clear and loud:

"If you have no mercy for the living," he said, "in common dacency ye might respect the dead. Lave me alone bhoys to-night

with me sorrow and I'll swear by the Virgin
that yez shall find me in the cabin alone
to-morrow night an' I'll not open me lips to a
sowl in the manewhile."

"It's purty fools you be takin' us for,
Terence Flynn," said the former speaker, with
a gruff laugh. "Would the fox come back
to the hen-roost the next night, if the farmer
let him go? Come down, I say, we've a question or two to ask you!"

Terence paused; and once more his eye
moved round the room : to go down that stair
was he knew to go to his doom. Ah! there was
the window, it would be easy for an active
man to drop from that to the ground; and,
though they had doubtless men on the watch
outside, yet he could trust to the fleetest foot
in the barony, if he once got safely through
them; his mother had been dead some hours,
life was sweet, and had he not Norah still to
take care of in this world? His mind was
made up; the living before the dead. They

would surely respect his mother's remains; he would try it.

"Two minutes, boys," he called out down the staircase. "Give me time to say one prayer by her bedside," and with that he crossed the room and opened the lattice.

"Troth; it would be hard to grudge him that," said Cassidy, with a brutal chuckle, " for if iver a man had need of a prayer, its Terence Flynn this minnit."

The ruffian little thought that he himself had more need to make his shrift than his intended victim.

Noiselessly, Flynn dropped from the window and stole along the shadow of the house. He could see no sentries, but guessed for all that they were there; he knew that he had no time to spare, for that his escape must be speedily discovered. He had made up his mind that Rathkelly was the nearest place where he could hope for refuge.

Cassidy, meanwhile, became impatient.

Though without any idea that his victim had escaped him. "You're a long time making your pace, I'm thinkin'," jeered the ruffian, "and we must throuble ye not to keep us waitin' much longer."

At this moment, Terence sprang out into the moonlight, and started like a deer straight across country for Rathkelly. As he had supposed, the cabin was watched from the outside, and before he had gone thirty yards, a man sprang from behind a hedge at no great distance, and immediately discharged a gun at him, which conveyed to his comrades inside an intimation that Terence had fled.

"Tare an' owns," thundered Cassidy, as he rushed up the staircase; "the divil has slipepd us." One glance round the chamber, one look at the open window, and the ruffian came blundering down again.

"Follow him, bhoys; follow him, and use your guns, bhoys. It'll niver do to let him go free now."

In an instant, the whole gang had poured out of the house, and after exchanging a hurried word with their sentries, started in hot pursuit. Cassidy, and one or two of his band, knew that their chance of coming up with Terence was slight, unless they could contrive to wound him. He was the best runner in the district, and though they could see him speeding along not above a hundred yards a-head, even Cassidy felt that the chance of any of his companions hitting Terence at that distance was slight. Suddenly an idea shot across his crafty brain; he knew the country as well as Terence did, and, from the direction the latter was heading, made no doubt but what Rathkelly Castle was his point. He would not blow his men, nor run the risk of arousing the district by any further firing; they should dog their prey at a distance, just to convince him that he was right in his surmise; and then, Cassidy thought, an hour before daybreak, they would

attack the Castle itself. What a grand blow
this would be to strike for the League! After
that, they would be bound to fill his pockets
and send him to America; he was getting
very tired of playing hide and seek with
the police in the mountains. Then, again,
the ruffian thought what a glorious vengeance
he would take on those he termed his foes,
Terence Flynn and the Master of Rathkelly:
he would settle scores with the two of them,
and if a stray shot should happen to put an
end to Norah Ryan; well, she would be re-
leased from a wicked world, and it would be
no great matter. They had only two men to
fear inside the house, even if they did'nt
manage to surprise them—Terence Flynn and
Mr. Eyre—and at thought of the Master
Mike Cassidy winced a little. There was a
deep-rooted tradition in the barony, that the
Eyres were dangerous to face in their hour of
wrath. As for the old butler, he did not
count for much; while O'Reilly, the hunts-

man, had been a cripple ever since the day
the hunt was boycotted at Ballater Gorse.
Mike Cassidy's descent of Avernus had been
rapid since we first met him. Then he was
a lazy, discontented farmer, neglecting his
business to dabble in politics. Now, thanks
to the inflammatory teaching of Messrs.
Carmody and Last, and their subordinates,
aggravated by indulgence in shebeen oratory
and unlimited whiskey, he had become a
murderous, drunken, unscrupulous ruffian.

CHAPTER XII.

BEFORE Terence had covered half the distance to Rathkelly Castle he discovered that he had outstripped his pursuers, and that when they were once aware of his destination they should dare to continue pursuit was a thing that never entered his head. That any party of Moonlighters who ever started in search of scalps should dare " to beard the lion in his den, the Master in his hold," was a thing past Terence's comprehension. The great problem to him was to obtain entrance to Rathkelly without disturbing the family. He had paid many a visit to his sweetheart since she had taken up her residence at the Castle. He knew

the window of her chamber, which was close
to her young mistress's room, and the question was, how to arouse Norah without
waking Miss Eyre or any other of the inmates. If he could do that, he might safely
count on shelter till morning, and pardon
for his intrusion when his story was told.
To tap at a window on the ground floor, or
to throw a handful of gravel at the required
casement should it be above, is the recognized
thing in such cases, with no harm likely to
come of it in an ordinary peaceable country,
but in a district suffering under "the Terror"
like that of Callowtown, it was quite possible
that the disturbed inmate, if of nervous temperament, might fire first, and ask what it
was that the would-be intruder wanted
afterwards. Old Flannigan, the butler, very
likely indeed, under existing circumstances,
to empty the family blunderbuss to start
with if abruptly aroused from his slumbers

Such considerations as these troubled

Terence but little, still, he did know that his
pursuers, if he had distanced them for the
present, were probably close upon his trail,
and that should he fail to obtain admittance to
the castle, he was as like to die *without* that
house as but many minutes before he had
been to do so *in* his own. Picking up a
handful of gravel he threw it lightly against
the casement of his betrothed with a result
he was hardly prepared for. Another window
was sharply thrown up, and a voice, which
Terence recognized at once, sternly demanded:

"What the devil do you want, and who
are you?"

"Terence   Flynn,   your   honour.   My
mother died to-night, Heaven rest her
sowl, and the Moonlighters are hunting me
this minute."

"Go round to the side door. I think I
can trust you, but remember, I shall
be armed, and if there's any sign of
treachery——"

" Niver moind the side door. Av ye think
that of me I'm best left outside. God for-
give your honour for thinking so badly of
me——"

" Do as I tell you, go round to the side
door," was the stern response, and Terence
bowed meekly to Mr. Eyre's decree, as most
of his tenants had been wont to, ere the
salvation of their country was preached to
them from New York.

Another moment, and the door in question
was opened, and very much to Terence's
astonishment, not by Mr. Eyre, but by
O'Reilly. The old huntsman, although crippled for life, was still as dauntless as in the
days when he followed straight in the wake of
his darlings. He and the Master had, so to
speak, rehearsed this scene previously, and
thoroughly settled in what manner that side
door should be opened. As Terence stepped
across the threshold into the full glare of
O'Reilly's lantern, he became conscious of

the figure of "the Masther" standing in the shadow and covering the door with a cocked revolver. Mr. Eyre might well give the caution "beware of treachery," for the leader of any attack of that nature would have to face the fire of as deadly a hand as ever drew trigger.

"Put up the bolts, O'Reilly, and now come up, Terence, and let one know what brought you here. You'll excuse my receiving you with all the honours," said Mr. Eyre, with a bitter laugh, "but we can't be certain of our visitors in these times. Now, what is it?"

"Shure the mother is lying dead in the old home, and I've had to fly for my loife. Cassidy's out at the head of a large party of Moonlighters. I'd have been a dead man this minnit av I hadn't given thim the slip and had the foot of them."

"And you've come here for refuge."

"That's so, your honour. I'd no wheres

else to go. They're too many intoirely, an' they've all guns."

"Very good, Terence. Of course, I'll stand by you if they follow you here——"

"Follow me here," cried Terence. "Och! they'd niver dare do that," and the young man looked at Mr. Eyre with undisguised amazement at the bare idea of such a thing.

"Perhaps not," replied Mr. Eyre. "I can only say you'll have to fight for your life like the rest of us if they do. Now, O'Reilly, show him some place to sleep."

Flynn followed the old huntsman, who had long since been moved away from his old quarters over the stables to a room which had been specially chosen as likely to contribute to the defence of the house. It was on the first floor, and its bay mullioned window, projecting a little, commanded a flank fire of the small door. Since the murder of Ryan, Mr. Eyre had put his house in quite a defensive state. A few months back it had

been easy to get into the house in a dozen
different ways, but now it was not so. Mr.
Eyre, wisely recognising that such a barrack
of a building could not possibly be defended
by so small a garrison, had, by bolt, bar and
barricade, cut off one wing of the house
completely from the rest, and to this citadel
the family now retreated at nightfall, and
were, the Master considered, in a position to
offer a stout resistance to any attack they
might reasonably expect. A feeble garrison
no doubt; but dauntless, with one exception,
and that was Norah Ryan. The poor girl
seemed utterly broken down by her troubles;
she struggled bravely against it, but her nerves
had not as yet recovered the shock of seeing
her father murdered before her eyes, while
she had suffered from the subsequent scene in
the chapel as any human being must suffer,
who is ruthlessly and shamefully cast out, not
only from the community but almost from
the very church itself. Even old Flannigan,

the butler, although not much to be counted
upon, was brim full of fight, and had been
allotted a fowling piece with which, as
the Master observed, "he might with luck
perhaps hit something." Had Mike Cassidy
known the preparations made for the recep-
tion of Moonlighters, he would probably have
reconsidered his determination of attacking
the castle.

Cassidy, having recalled his followers from
their pursuit of Terence, proceeded back to
the cabin, tenanted now only by the dead
woman. There, after rummaging about until
they had found Terence's modest store of
whisky, they sat down, and Cassidy unfolded
his scheme. He expatiated upon the weakness of the garrison, and upon the tremendous
effect such an attack would have. "It's not
just punishing a tinant, bhoys, but it's
punishing a landlord for daring to receive
thim," but despite his arguments there was
considerable demur amongst his followers at

the idea of attacking the castle. His band, as
before said, consisted chiefly of men from a
distance, but there were two or three who came
from around Callowtown, and these it was
who did not seem to fancy facing the Master
of Rathkelly.

"It's loike to be a tough job," said one of
them doggedly. "The Eyres have ever
been ill to meddle with. Ould Eyre will die
like a fox, foighting, an' he'll lave his marks
on some of us, niver fear."

The speaker had made an impression, and
Cassidy saw with unconcealed dissatisfaction,
that he had done so, but, like so many of us,
Murphy did not recognise when he had said
enough. He did'nt know when to stop.

"Besides," he continued, "if we put a
man like Eyre of Rathkelly out of the way,
they'll raise such a hue and cry all through
country side we'll be hunted down."

"To the devil with yer doubts," interrupted Cassidy roughly. "Ye've about as

much heart, Murphy, as a soft-roed herring
D'ye think any of thim can raise the counthry
or scour the mountains like him ye've
just mentioned. Ye may trust my word for
that," said the ruffian, with a brutal laugh.
" Ye may take my word for that ; and, by
the powers, Moike Cassidy ought to know."

There were meaning glances exchanged
between the men. There was not one among
them who did not know how fiercely hunted
Cassidy had been in the last few weeks ; and,
that Ratcliffe Eyre had been the life and
soul of that fierce pursuit. Murphy's speech
recoiled upon himself ; and Cassidy had shown
good cause why a blow should be struck at
the Master of Rathkelly. It turned the scale,
and it was voted by a large majority that
Cassidy's scheme should be carried out.

" We'll not need to start till the moon is
down," said that ruffian ; " and, in the meantime, this is moighty pleasant whiskey of
Misther Flynn's. Don't spare it, bhoys. It's

not loikely the family will have much further use for it," and Mr. Cassidy indulged in a boisterous laugh at his own brutal jest.

The moon was down, and it wanted, still, close upon two hours of day-break, when, flushed with whiskey, Cassidy and his half-drunken band set forth for the castle. There was some slight inclination amongst his followers to indulge in ribald jest and laughter, which was promptly checked by their leader, in the first instance—and the recollection of their errand, in the second. Should they fail to surprise the Master of Rathkelly, there was a general feeling that— terminate as it might—there would be no such one-sided battle as they were accustomed to; and that some of themselves, as well as their victims, might be stark and stiff when the sun rose. Piloted by their leader and those belonging to the district, they made their way swiftly and stealthily over the ground that intervened between

Flynn's cottage and their destination. The house was all in darkness. The closest inspection failed to discover any sign of a life within the mansion. The inmates were apparently all locked in slumber, and little apprehensive of such a thing as a night-attack.

" 'Tis as I thought, bhoys," whispered Cassidy. " Auld Eyre, in his moightiness, never drames we'd dare favour his worship with a call. Flynn's in there, we know, and we have got to have him out ; and when we have lain him and his landlord out on the lawn here, maybe folks will understand they'd best not quarrel with the League."

But how to get in ? That—if they only found the inmates asleep—there could be any difficulty about this had never occurred to Cassidy, or those who knew the ways of Rathkelly Castle. They were perfectly unaware of how the house had been barricaded of late, and many a window on the ground-

floor--which they had looked upon as offering
easy access—was now found, not only bolted
and barred, but evidently closed also with
thick heavy planking inside.

Cassidy knew the house perhaps as well as
any of them ; and after listening attentively
to the report of his scouts, said :

" There's only the one way, bhoys! Ye
moight as well kick against the gates of
Callowtown goal, as thry the front door ; but
the side door, opening on to the garden,
that's just the place we'll have 'em ! I've
noticed the boults and the locks there,
many's the toime! and they were just good
enough never to think of strengthening —
and just bad enough to be niver a bit
of use when anny one meant to smash the
doors in ! Take a look round some of yez !
Maybe ye'll find a pole of some sort ! that'll
do to drive the door in with. If not Murphy
and one or two of yez have hatchets—cut me
down a young tree and bring it here."

Still in spite of the stealthy attempt on the windows, in spite of the low whispering in front of the house, there was no sign of life within the building, and yet for all that quick ears and keen, pitiless eyes, were noting every preliminary movement of the assailants.

Ratcliffe Eyre, having dismissed the old huntsman and Terence to their slumbers, had taken upon himself to keep watch and ward for the night. That Terence had failed to awaken Norah was attributed to the circumstance that, under the new arrangements, her room had been changed. Mr. Eyre, whose restlessness in these days knew no bounds, was the one person who heard Terence's signal, and having aroused O'Reilly, he admitted him in the manner we have seen. He did not believe that the Moonlighters would dare to attack Rathkelly, but he was not going to throw a chance away, and his pulses quickened at the bare idea of having it out face to face with Mike Cassidy.

Mike Cassidy was cunning as a fox. He had
been perfectly right in his conjecture and
that the weakness of the lock and bolts of the
side door had been somwhat overlooked by
Mr. Eyre when putting his house in a state of
defence. It was not that they had escaped
his eye altogether, but he thought that they
would serve for the present. As for knock-
ing and demanding entrance, Cassidy knew
the Master better than that. To knock would
be to arouse the inmates, the reply he felt
sure would be a shot. The extreme silence
and the darkness in which the house was
shrouded, gave him hopes of effecting a
surprise. His scheme was to dash in the
door with his improvised battering ram,
rush up stairs and capture the little garrison
before they were fairly aroused from their
slumbers. He was however very far out in
his calculations. The Moonlighters had
hardly made their appearance on the lawn
which ran on the west side of the house,

before Ratcliffe Eyre discovered them. His
preparations for an attack of this sort had
been already determined; the one light in
the house was in a bath-room off his own
chamber. Rapidly and silently he went from
room to room and roused his household, what
each was to do in case of this emergency had
long ago been settled, and both men and
women repaired armed to their respective posts,
Even Katie carried a light fowling-piece.

Mr. Eyre's orders were imperative. "Not
a light to be shown, not a shot to be fired
till I give the orders. Then, from where I
have placed you, keep up a fire on those
trying to break into the house until you hear
from me. We must not make the mistake of
firing until we have a clear case of burglary
against them." For himself the Master had
reserved a roving commission, and with a
revolver in one hand and a dark lantern in
the other, besides a second revolver thrust
into a silk handkerchief round his waist,

the Master looked a very awkward customer
to intrude upon without his own consent.
Mr. Eyre's room had two windows. The one
jutted out, and commanded a flank view of
the small door, the other looked out over
the lawn on the west side the mansion, and
it was from this latter that the Master stood
watching as well as he could the proceedings
of the Moonlighters. He could not see them
very well at first, but could make out that
they were somewhat puzzled at finding the
doors and windows of the house so well
secured. They were doubtless, he thought,
holding council among themselves about
what they should do. They would probably
decide that breaking into Rathkelly was a
stiffer nut to crack than they had thought
it; but no, they showed no signs of going
away. What could they be waiting for.
The mystery is soon solved. Four of the
assailants, bearing amongst them a young
tree, join the main body.

"Damnation!" exclaimed Ratcliffe Eyre, "I never thought of that. The bolts and bars will never stand it." One more glance and his resolution was taken. Quick as thought he ran down the stairs, placed the lantern in an angle of the wall, and drew back the slide, so that the light should fall full upon the sill the moment the door should be burst in. It was the same tactics he had resorted to in admitting Terence Flynn, only against a crowd of men he would not let O'Reilly run the risk of carrying the lantern. There was an ominous silence for some few minutes outside, he could hear a low murmuring of voices from where he stood in the shadow some few steps up the staircase, then a hoarse low voice exclaimed: "Now, bhoys, all together!"

There was a quick rush of footsteps and the young tree was crashed against the door, bolts and bars were shivered like touchwood, and the entrance to Rathkelly is won.

30*

"Fire!" thundered Ratcliffe Eyre from his coign of vantage, and three or four shots were discharged from the upper windows which, together with their hardly expected success, somewhat checked the rush of the marauders. "Forward!" shouted their leader as he sprang towards the stairs.

Clear as a clarion Ratcliffe Eyre's voice rose above the din. "Shot for shot, Mike Cassidy," he exclaimed, "and may the Lord have mercy upon your soul!" The crack of the Master's revolver rang through the air and Cassidy fell back with a bullet through his brain.

CHAPTER XIII.

" GOOD-BYE TO RATHKELLY."

Cowed by the fall of their leader, with two or three of their number wounded by the unexpected fire from the upper windows, and startled to find the household most completely prepared to receive them, Cassidy's followers shrank back. To hesitate under those circumstances meant to be beaten; again the deadly revolver twice rang out from the staircase and another of the assailants felt his arm scored by a bullet. It is enough, the Moonlighters recoil, another shot or two from the upper windows quickened their pace, and in another minute or two their retreat bade fair to degenerate

into a "*sauve qui peut*," and when the sun
rose, the shattered doorway and the corpse of
Mike Cassidy stretched prone in the passage
were the sole traces left of an attack which,
but for the precautions and watchfulness of
the Master, might have found Rathkelly the
scene of as sanguinary a holocaust as ever
stained the South of Ireland.

Mr. Eyre and Terence stood side by side
looking at the dead man.

"It's no mercy your honour, he deserved at
either your hands or mine. It's no fault of
his I'm not lying like himself at my own
threshold, and though it's mere guess-work
on my part, I'm thinking ye'd niver have
reached home that day ye were up before
the magisthrates if his hand had been as thrue
as yer honour's."

"You're right, Terence, I have good
reason to believe it was 'shot for shot' and
Mike Cassidy had his first. And now off you
go to the police-station, tell them all about

this, and say the officer had better come up at once. These rascals have been too roughly handled to think about anything but saving their own skins for the present. There are two or three of them badly marked. As for you, you had better take up your quarters here. There is plenty of room, and though I don't think they will dare pay *you* another visit, it's no use risking it."

The officer soon arrived at the castle in obedience to Mr. Eyre's message.

"Ah, sir," he said as he looked at the traces of the fray. "I urged you to put yourself under our protection."

"Upon my soul," laughed Ratcliffe Eyre, "I think we've done pretty fairly without it. There lies the murderer we've been scouring the country for for weeks. I felt it was a duel to the death between us and it's over you see."

At that instant Katie and her foster-sister made their appearance.

"Papa," she said, "scold this foolish girl for me, and tell her not to talk nonsense."

"What is it?" enquired Mr. Eyre.

"Oh, she is talking all sorts of nonsense of how she brings death and sorrow on all she comes across."

"Look!" cried Norah, covering her face after glancing for an instant at the dead man; "there's another. I must leave you all. Good-bye, Mr Eyre and thank you kindly, but it's blood, all blood, I walk through it— I carry it with me—it will be your turn next Terence dear, maybe — God knows. My poor head, I can hear the shots still. It's Mike Cassidy leading them. He'll show no mercy."

"Take her to bed," said Mr. Eyre sternly. "You ought to have known better, Katie, than to let her be still about. The girl's distraught. It's all been too much for her. Her nerves have given way altogether."

"But papa, dear, I didn't know."

"Flurried yourself a bit, no doubt. Terence take your sweetheart away and hand her over to her mother. By Heavens! these are no times for women to face," cried Eyre, as the girls, escorted by Terence, retired.

"My daughter has lots of pluck, but her eyes are bolting out of her head this morning. No wonder, after last night's work. If the house had been unprepared and the shooting not pretty straight, how many of us do you think would have seen the sun rise?"

"I can't say," replied the officer gravely, "but I doubt whether either yourself or Flynn would."

"No fear," replied the Master of Rathkelly, with a grim smile. "We fought for our lives, as I mean some of my last night's visitors to do still. There are two or three winged birds to pick up yet."

Mr. Barton rubbed his hands. He was a thoroughly good-hearted man, but it is

the instinct of the police officer to track the
criminal, as it is that of the lawyer to press
for a conviction, or the hound to strain on
the trail of his quarry.

Mr. Eyre was a magistrate who had of late
aroused much reverence in his breast. His
dauntless courage and untiring energy had
made a great impression on Mr. Barton;
and with Mr. Eyre's assistance he felt very
sanguine of bringing the offenders to justice.
In this, however, it may be at once said the
officer was doomed to disappointment. The
great body of the Moonlighters had come from
a distance, and the two or three of the band
who lived in the neighbourhood had not been
recognised by either Terence or the Master
of Rathkelly. The wounded, whether badly
hurt or not, had contrived to get off, and
were by this in all probability spirited out
of the immediate district; but if both police
and magistrates were thoroughly baffled and
could lay their hands on no one to call to

account for the Rathkelly outrage, yet the
Leaguers, and especially McDermot, were
much disconcerted at the results of their
coup. They had meant to strike a blow
which should paralyse the action of the
Government, and make them afraid to use
the powers so lately conferred upon them by
Parliament.

They were mistaken: for the first time they
found the Crimes Act firmly, though fairly,
carried out, and soon awoke to the fact that
the half-hearted administration which had
characterised the authorities in the use of
such powers formerly was by no means the
manner in which the present men intended
carrying them out. Not only was the district
proclaimed, but shebeen politicians, like
Mr. McDermot, and also their illustrious
representatives with seats at St. Stephen's,
were made clearly to understand that
although the right of public meeting was
by no means suspended, yet that public meet-

ing for the promotion of illegal purposes
would no longer be tolerated, and that inflammatory speeches, tending to produce a
breach of the peace, would infallibly result
in the speedy imprisonment of the offender.
There was one weapon left to the myrmidons
of Messrs. Last and Carmody, and McDermot
speedily issued a ukase of proscription
against Ratcliffe Eyre and all within the walls
of Rathkelly, a decree pronounced by the
Head of the Roman Catholic Church as
contrary to the laws of God and man.

Ratcliffe Eyre smiled grimly when he
found that he was boycotted, but he had
not as yet fully recognised the iron tyranny
of the League, and could not have believed
that not a tenant on his estate dared supply
him with milk, butter, eggs, etc. He and his
might have starved for all the supplies he
could have procured in his own neighbourhood; the very shopkeepers in Callowtown,
with whom he had dealt for years, looked

askance at any inmate of his house, and if
they served him, did so by stealth.

He was in no danger of starvation, for the
authorities were quite as resolute in the
support of law and order as the League in
their subversion. Provisions were forwarded
regularly from a distance, and the police took
good care that these safely reached their
destination; and as the Master of Rathkelly
remarked to Jack Blake, who, in spite of the
menacing missives that had been sent him,
had ridden over to see his old friend :

"There's stuff enough in the cellars to
stand a five years' siege. But the sentence
of excommunication is as hard to struggle
against as in the days of King John." A few
months back and he had been almost a mis-
anthrope, caring for no other society than
that of his daughter Katie, but the arrival of
Mrs. Belton and the coming of Sturton to
Conroy, had roused him considerably, and
the excitement caused by his untiring efforts

to avenge Ryan's murder, had supplied the
stimulant he wanted. He felt desire now to
mix again with his fellows, to, in sober
fashion, resume the pursuits of his younger
days; but, except a few old friends like
Blake, he saw nobody, and he knew that
even these had received warning that he was
proscribed, and that they had been threatened
with a like fate should they dare to hold
intercourse with him. Shooting and fishing
are poor fun when prosecuted under a guard
of policemen, and the end of it was that
Ra'cliffe Eyre got very much bored with the
situation. Katie, too, was beginning to look
worn with the strain that had been lately put
upon her, and as for Norah, although she
had recovered from her light-headedness, she
was pitiably broken down in nerves and
general health, and Doctor Connolly said point
blank : " I can do no more 'for her. She will
never recover here ; she wants complete
change of scene and the assurance that she is

beyond the power of the Land League. Here
her mind conjures up some new danger, day
and night, and though, as 1 honestly believe,
Mr. Eyre, there is not a house in the country
less likely to be meddled with again than
yours, you will never make her think that."

Mr. Eyre was a man of decision. His mind
was soon made up. " The hounds are gone,
and the horses too, pretty well. The three
that are left I will send up to Dycer's. I'll
lock up this old barrack, leave my agent to
manage things for me, and I'll take a small
cottage near London. God knows what I
shall do when I get there. There'll be little
enough left to keep the lot of us, and I don't
know what I'm fit for even if I wasn't almost
too old to get anything. Now comes the
question. What am I to do with these two
old men? Mrs. Flynn and Norah are all the
servants we shall want. I can't cut Flannigan
adrift, so I suppose he'll have to come with us ;
but what can I do with O'Reilly? The poor

old man is too crippled to do a day's work
either in the saddle or anywhere else. I must
talk to Jack Blake about it."

As for Katie, she heard with dismay her
father's idea of abandoning Rathkelly and
migrating to the vicinity of London. She
puckered up her pretty brows and listened
with earnest attention as Mr. Eyre proceeded
to explain to her the painfully diminished
state of his income. "To live here as I used
to do in the days when you were a little
thing has been long impossible, but I tell you
of late things have been so bad, it's getting
hard work to live here at all. What I must
try and do is this. Let the old place if I can
—it's worth somebody's while to take for
the sake of the shooting and fishing—the
people here will have no object in interfering with a stranger who comes for that
purpose. The land, the rents and the leases
will be no business of his, and we ought to
get enough for it to be a considerable help

to us in England. As for the horses, they must go."

" What! not Rory, papa——"

" Yes, indeed, Rory and all. It is a case my dear, now, of living, not luxuries."

" Oh, papa ! " cried Katie, " I never thought to part with Rory as long as he lived. Don't speak to me any more now, I want to think it all out. To leave my old home is bad enough, but to part with my pet horse is worse. I'm not afraid of being poor, you know that," and with these words, Katie slipped out of the room.

It is ever so ; when that miserable cry of retrenchment comes to us, there is always some superfluity, the abandonment of which wrings our withers harder than all the rest. Similarly too, a thing which we have had at our command half our lifetime, and never desired, we suddenly conceive a longing for, when we find it all at once beyond our reach.

Katie went straight to her own room, drew

her pet chair to the window and sat down to think things seriously over. Poor, she wondered, how poor. She asserted no more than the truth, when she said she was not afraid of being poor; but she dearly loved her father, and the thought that he at his age might have to do without the comforts that he had been all his life accustomed to, troubled the girl greatly. What could she do to prevent this; money, money, she must earn money, but how? What could she do, that people would pay her to do it. Yes, she supposed she could make a good housemaid if she set resolutely to work; but then housemaids could hardly be said to make money. She was no good with her needle, besides women did not make money by that. She was no fool, she could sing a little and play a little, had a smattering of languages, but she knew very well that she was not fitted to teach even the smattering she knew to anyone else. And

Rory! Of course he must go. If they had barely money to live upon, how could they afford to keep a horse? Money! money, again, what could she do to earn money, and once more severely and critically Katie went through the small roll of her accomplishments. "No," she said ruefully at last, "I can make money at none of these things, I can do nothing but ride." Suddenly her face lit up. "Ride! ah, why shouldn't I teach that. I don't know how much, but I do know that both in Dublin and London ladies pay for riding lessons, and I do think I have heard pay pretty well. I think that might do. Yes if I can only manage to get pupils, Rory and I might earn enough to keep ourselves and help papa too," and springing to her feet. the girl clapped her hands and then rushed off in her own impetuous fashion to intercede in Rory's behalf with her father.

"Papa dear," she cried as she rushed into her father's sanctum, where Mr. Eyre sat busy at a table covered with papers, "you've told me the horses must all go, even Rory. I want you to do this for me, let us take Rory across to London, you will be able to sell him quite as well there, as in Dublin, will you not?"

"I should think so; probably better, they've more money there Katie, than we have here."

"And it won't cost very much to take him across."

"No, nothing worth considering," said Mr. Eyre, in the easy tone of a man still unused to the consideration of such minor details.

"Then papa, I want you to promise that we shall take Rory with us, and if before he has been three months in London, he is not earning his own living, then I'll not say a word against his being sold."

"Why, what on earth are you thinking of Katie," exclaimed her father. "You can't set up a hansom cab on your own account, you know. However, you shall have your wish, upon one condition—that is, you let me know

as soon as you find your scheme is hopeless.
Horses cost a good deal to keep in London,
remember."

" Thanks, papa dear," said the girl, kissing
him, and highly elated at this idea that had
occurred to her, Katie next ran off to tell
Norah they were all going to leave Rathkelly.

Norah's face flushed with pleasure and her
eyes sparkled at the news. She had no
regrets at leaving her old home; that, and
the district in which she had been born and
bred, were accursed in her eyes.

She knew herself surrounded by men who
had shed her father's blood, who thirsted for
her lover's, and at whose bidding sentence of
excommunication had been passed against
herself; men whose bitter enmity and callous-
ness to crime had even led them to attack
Rathkelly. The girl had been very ill, and
two or three days after the attack on the
castle, had wandered a great deal in her

talk. Though better, she was still far from convalescent, and the doctor declared a complete change of scene would do far more for her recovery than anything else.

" Going to lave Rathkelly, Miss Katie. What all of us ? "

" Yes. Papa and I are going to live near London, and you, your mother, and Flannigan are to come with us."

" And Terence, Miss Katie, shure you'll take him too ? "

" He will come across with us, Norah, but papa and I are very poor now ; he will have to take care of himself."

" Oh, he'll do that, niver fear," said the girl brightly. " He's sent away all his stock and sold it, indeed except for me, he'd have been gone before this. The League won't let him live here."

" Ah, well, that's all settled. And now all you've got to do is to set to work and grow strong."

"An' I'm not to lave you, Miss Katie. I'm so glad, an' I'll thry me best to get well and help as quick as possible."

"Mind you do," said Miss Eyre, as she kissed her patient."

CHAPTER XIV.

" WHAT'S BREACH OF PRIVILEGE ? "

THE Callowtown Committee of The League were not a little dismayed at the utter defeat of their emissaries. They had intended to confound the Government by their audacity, to show them that the Crimes Act, far from suppressing, simply increased crime. Cassidy had gone beyond his instructions. The idea was magnificent! it was sublime! After being foiled in his attempt to assassinate Flynn by the latter's flight it was a great and daring conception to think of plucking him forth to meet his doom from the sanctuary of Rathkelly Castle. Successful, Michael Cassidy would have stood forth as one of the saviours of his oppressed country. As it was, he had laid down his life in its behalf, and it behoved all good patriots to pray for the soul of the martyr. Such was the bombastic language used by the organs of the League, and those minor lights of oratory, Messrs. McDermot and Co. Nevertheless, they could not disguise from themselves that the tyranny which they had so rapidly built up in County Blarney, bid fair to tumble to pieces with almost similar celerity. The fungus is both noxious and of quick growth, but it is short-lived and very perishable. The steady patrolling of police and soldiers through the country was making moonlighting as dangerous to those who practised it as to those on whom it was practised. Open air meetings were attended in force by the police as well as the patriot, and those reckless and inflammatory harangues, in which Messrs. Carmody and Last were wont to indulge, promptly interfered with. The orator of the platform found himself at length held responsible for the effect of his words.

It might be all very well to represent Cassidy as a martyr who died for the cause, but around Callowtown, where Ryan had been well known, it was hard to make the people consider him anything but a brutal ruffian who had met his deserts for one murder in attempting to commit a second.

"It's a despotism worse than Russian," said Mr. McDermot, "when a few gentlemen can't convane themselves under the blue vault of heaven, for the exchange of political sentiments" —here the speaker looked round for applause—" at all events," he resumed, " I presume the police, the blackgairds can't interfere with our takin' a glass of punch together."

Mr. McDermot, finding the use of violent language in the open air was at present attended with unpleasant results, had called together a meeting of the leading Nationalists

of his district at his own house, where liberty
of speech was not what he called " resthricted,"
which meant that the most violent and sedi-
tious language could be used with impunity.
One great object was to rebuke the people
generally for remissness in subscribing to the
funds of the League. Secondly, to appease a
spirit of discontent that was rapidly spread-
ing amongst the peasantry " We must stand
shoulther to shoulther in the prisent crisis
an' we'll soon get our own again."

What the speaker had meant exactly by
this latter sentiment he would have been
much puzzled to explain, but Mr. McDermot,
like many other patriots, was remarkably
fond of hearing his own voice. "Now,
Murphy, you for one, I'm tould, have been
grumbling at the state of things ! Is is thrue
ye said we'd have done betther not to do
away with the hounds."

" It's just that I'm thinking," replied the
accused : " the toimes was hard thin, but

money was more plentiful annyway, before
we druv them out of the counthry. The
gontlemen of the Harkhallow spent a power
of money amongst us; av we paid ould
Eyre for his land, he paid us for what we
grew on it!"

"Howld your wisht, Pat Murphy; I'm
downright ashamed of ye. Where's yez
patriotism I'd be glad to know?"

"Where yours would be," retorted Mr.
Murphy, "av ye weren't paid for it."

This bold remark was received with rather
varied views by the little meeting. About
half of them were on the Callowtown Committee, and by these the speaker was regarded
with considerable disfavour. To sneer at
the patriotism of the League, or make light
of its authority, would never do. There were
snug little pickings to be had by those who
once got their hand in the money bags. On
the other hand, that half the meeting who
were not upon the committee, sympathised

with Murphy, and chuckled considerably at
his sharp retort. For a moment, McDermot was
disconcerted, and taking advantage thereof
his opponent continued; "When we paid
our rints to Misther Eyre they came back to
us more or less ; when we pay them to the
League they don't come back, whativer else
becomes of them ?"

Once again there was a murmur of
applause, and a voice exclaimed : "There was
at all evints some business in those toimes,
there's divil a bit now," but the blustering.
McDermot rose to the occasion. He felt he had
caught a Tartar. He was quite aware that
this same Murphy, far from being actually
hostile to the League, had taken part in the
attack upon Flynn's cottage, and afterwards
on Rathkelly. He, indeed, was the man who
had raised a protest against attempting the
castle, which Cassidy had successfully com-
bated.

"If it's for funning ye are, Misther Murphy,

I'll not baulk ye! What's the use of talking serious to a man who's dyin' for his joke. We'll just lave the discussion at present, and discuss, bhoys, the subject on which Irishmen differ but little, and that's the punch. Punch is moighty like politics, bhoys, some loikes it with one lump of sugar, some loikes it with two."

"Bedad, if ye loike your punch loike your politics, McDermot, it's a good three you'll be takin'," said Murphy. This allusion to the current report that McDermot was the well-paid servant of the League, was received with a broad grin, and more than ever convinced McDermot of his prudence in putting politics on one side for the present.

*   *   *   *   *

"What's going on inside?" enquired his fidus Achates of the Honourable Augustus Danby as that exceedingly bored young gentleman, lounged into the smoking-room of the House of Commons, towards the very end of the session.

"How about breach of privilege," was the reply, as Mr. Danby threw himself down upon the sofa by his friend, and proceeded to light a cigarette. "Never can make out what the deuce they mean by breach of privilege myself."

"Can't you," rejoined his friend drily. "Just one of the few things I do understand. Look here, I'll explain it in a minute. I call you a liar in Bond Street; you knock me down, which is all in the nature of things. I call you a liar in the House of Commons; you knock me down and it's a breach of privilege."

"License to use bad language, I am gradually beginning to understand, our senatorial privileges."

"And that's more than some of these fellows do their sartorial responsibilities," returned his friend. "Can't think

myself where the deuce they get such
coats."

Eminent orator meanwhile in the chamber
is fluently assuring his hearers that what he
is reported to have said two or three years
ago has been grossly misrepresented, and
further what he really said has been painfully
misunderstood. He then further sets to work
with untiring assiduity to the ungrateful task
of washing the blackamoor white, and bespat-
tering the unsullied ermine of the Bench,
and although those who hear him may deplore
the direction his rhetoric has taken, yet all
must admit that there is no diminishing of
the old fire, and that the passionate declama-
tion flows as freely from his lips as in days of
yore.

Ratcliffe Eyre has carried out his resolution;
he has torn up his old life by the roots, left
Rathkelly behind him, and established himself and family in a small cottage at Hampstead. Mrs. Ryan and Norah sufficed to do

the work of the house, and Flannigan, though, as Mr. Eyre admits, a superfluity, relinquishing his butler's position once so tenaciously adhered to, has descended to boot-cleaning. Of the whole household none of them so conscious of their fallen fortunes as Mr. Flannigan. He had no longer even his old crony, Mrs. Martin, to grumble to, and had always accustomed himself to look down upon the Ryans, arguing " that it wasn't dacent for upper-servants to demane themselves with mere tinantry."

Katie cared little for the smallness of their means, although, as her father was obliged to confide to her, his income was reduced to an extent he had never even contemplated; but she was worried too. She was beginning to discover however good the wares you may have to sell the difficulty there is of finding a market for them in modern Babylon. She had perfectly made up her mind that the sole way in which she could earn money was by riding. It was, to use her own expression, "the one thing I'm good at." And the only way she saw to utilising that accomplishment was by teaching ladies to ride. Even if she had had a connection it would have been impossible for her to start upon her own account; that would require a regular establishment, horses, grooms, etc., and she, she had no capital, only Rory, and her own skill and pluck to depend upon. Again and again did she call at livery stable keepers' and at riding schools to ask if they could give her employment as a riding mistress. They listened civilly and attentively to what she had to say, but one and all shook their heads, and regretted that they were unable to help her to a situation such as she sought. The girl had been clever, too. She had called mounted on Rory, and attired in the most workmanlike hat and habit. If she could not get a berth for herself, she was often asked to put a price upon her horse, and

upon more than one occasion had been bid
what she regarded as a good price for him.
Katie was in despair; she could not bear the
idea of parting with Rory, and yet unless she
could get something to do it must be so.
The expense of a horse standing at livery in
London was a serious consideration when
household expenses had to be closely
calculated.

Suddenly a queer idea came into her head
which, for a moment, crimsoned her cheeks.

"I don't care," she said, "there can be no
harm in it. I've known him from a child
and there is nobody else to help me. Papa
has not been in London for so long that he
knows little more about it than I do, while
as for George Belton, I don't like to ask him,
for one thing, and I know he wouldn't help
me if I did. He would ask me to come
down and stay with them at Aldershot and
bring Rory, as if that was any good. I want
to make money. No; I'd rather apply to

Captain Sturton than George; he is more likely to help me, and if he tries, there's little he wouldn't succeed in," and then Katie, in her own impetuous fashion, rushed to her desk and sat down to write her letter.

"DEAR CAPTAIN STURTON," she began, and then for a minute or two the girl bit her pen and wondered how she was to go on. This letter was not quite so easy to write as she had fancied before she sat down. At last the inspiration seemed to seize her; she dipped her pen in the ink and dashed off her note without further hesitation. "I appeal to you as an old friend of my family and because I am in sore need of advice. But I must ask you, in the first place, to think of me no longer as a child. Remember, I am in my eighteenth year, and that the troubles we have gone through lately have been calculated to transform a girl into a woman in a very short time. You have heard of the

attack upon Rathkelly, and how we had to
fight for our very lives; only that papa had
taken the precautions to have the house well
barricaded it is impossible to say what might
have happened. It is needless to tell you
that we are in very reduced circumstances.
You know our part of Ireland too well not
to understand that under the reign of the
League no landlord can hope to get his rents.
I want to earn money. I want you, if you
can, to put me in the way of doing so. Can
you recommend me as riding mistress in a
riding school? What sort of a horsewoman
I am you know, and I can promise you that
I will not flinch from work. One thing more
—you will say I have neither patience nor
temper to turn schoolmistress, but ah!
Captain Sturton, believe me, late events have
sobered me completely. If you can help me in
this, I know you will. Papa is well, and bears
our changed circumstances a great deal better
than I could have hoped, but Flannigan cannot

forget the 'splendours of Rathkelly.' As for
poor O'Reilly, we left him behind. Mr. Blake
promised to take care of him, and without
his hounds, I fancy one place is much the
same to him as another. Hoping to hear
from you soon, and assuring you I am ter-
ribly in earnest about this scheme, believe me
with kind regards from us both,

" Yours most sincerely,

" KATIE EYRE."

When Sturton received this letter he was
more struck by Katie Eyre than he had ever
been yet. He had admired her hot-headed
courage when she boldly confronted the mob
that day at Ballater Gorse, but this was
a courage that men of Harold Sturton's
temperament put a much higher value upon
than that fiery daring that men display when
their blood is up and their pulse is stirred.
" It is one thing," he would say, " to take a big
fence when hounds are literally flying before

you, it is another thing to jump a six-foot
wall in cold blood. That girl is grit to the
back-bone, she don't whimper but faces the
change in her fortunes as pluckily as any
woman can do. Nothing mercenary about
her either, no other girl in her place would
have turned up her nose at Tom Chester
a good fellow and a good match for her.
Well I think I can do her a real turn here.
Ripley is under considerable obligations to
me, I should think his school is one of the
very best in town; if he can't give or find her
the berth she want's there's no one in London
can."

CHAPTER XV.

KATIE speedily received a reply to her letter. It was plain, straight-forward and to the point. He expressed regret but no surprise at their altered circumstances, and said how pleased he was to find they bore their misfortunes so bravely.

"You are quite right," he continued, " when the luck goes against us in this way the only thing is to face it and help ourselves. You want to make money, and, I think, have rightly selected the way in which you can do it best. I need scarcely say I am sorry the necessity has arisen, otherwise there are many Irish ladies more to be pitied than you at present. Teaching riding is, I should think, as pleasant an occupation as you could have hit upon. You will find it a little monotonous, all work is, and teaching in particular, but I should think the line you've picked out less than any. If you will take the enclosed letter to its address, Ripley will help you if he can, I am sure, and I know he'll stretch a point or two to oblige me. If he can't do it I don't know who to go to, but I trust he can. With kind regards to your father. Believe me, dear Miss Eyre,

"Most sincerely yours,

"HAROLD STURTON.

"P. S. I have unholy regrets that I was not in the fight at Rathkelly. Like your father I had a reckoning to settle with Mike Cassidy. However, he seems to have been paid in full."

Armed with this missive, Katie proceeded at once to Mr. Ripley's establishment at

Paddington. Mr. Ripley was a livery stable keeper on a large scale, and supplied the public with carriages and riding horses freely as long as they could pay for them. He had an extensive connection and did a very good business. Attached to his establishment was a large riding-school, and that also was a very thriving concern. Mr. Ripley never lacked well-to-do pupils, and many of the young ladies who figured in Rotten Row had gone through their novitiate at Ripley's. Not that that gentleman taught himself, but he had competent masters who undertook that duty. Mr. Ripley read Sturton's note attentively and then looked Katie over with a critical but approving eye. Miss Eyre had ridden from Hampstead, as was her custom, in search of the situation she required. Like most of his calling Ripley was a bit of a horse-dealer, and after his brief examination of the rider, his eye travelled with undisguised admiration over the horse.

"The Captain has been a good friend to me," he replied at length, "and I'd always go a good bit out of my way to oblige him. Now, Miss, a man don't want half an eye to see you can ride, and the Captain is not the man to send you to me on this errand if you couldn't. Would you mind coming into the school right off, there's a class on now. Just let me see you take your place amongst them and see how you manage a horse. Daresay neither you nor your horse were ever in a school before?"

"No," replied Katie, and then Mr. Ripley forthwith led the way into the riding-school.

Rory was a temperate horse, and therefore Miss Eyre had no trouble in keeping the place assigned to her amongst the other young ladies.

At the termination of the lesson, Mr. Ripley came forward and said:

"Now, Miss Eyre, just for form's sake, I should like to see you over the hurdles. If you can't trust your own horse, have one of mine."

" My own is a thoroughly broken hunter," said Katie, smiling.

" The big hurdles, or the little," asked Ripley.

" The big," rejoined Miss Eyre, determined to run no risks of losing an appointment for want of displaying her talent.

The big hurdles were accordingly put up, no very alarming leaps to a girl like Katie, accustomed to figure in the first flight across country. Rory negotiated them in faultless fashion, amidst a murmur of applause from the young ladies who had just dismounted, and were grouped around the door to witness the performance.

" Capital, Miss Eyre," exclaimed Ripley, as he walked forward into the centre of the school. " Now," he continued, lowering his voice, " I think I can promise to do what you want. There is no more doubt, of course,

about your being able to ride than there is
about your horse being able to jump. It
isn't that—but one may be able to do a
thing, and yet not be able to teach it.
Business is business. If you will ride in the
school for a fortnight, and pay close attention
to the riding master whatever you may
think, I can nearly promise you a situation,
as riding mistress. I want one to accompany
my more advanced pupils in the Park. One
thing I must point out to you :—Some young
ladies sit their horse gracefully from the
very first, and are no trouble; while
others require incessant correction for a long
time. I want your eye to get trained to
that."

It was accordingly settled that Katie
should ride in the school for a fortnight, and
if, at the end of that time, she gave satisfaction, she was to be appointed riding
mistress at a fixed salary.

Katie had great determination, and though

she chafed occasionally, at being pulled up
and checked by the riding-master, she resolutely kept her lips shut, and at the end of
the fortnight was pronounced one of the most
docile pupils that had ever been through the
school ; and her instructor was not a little
puzzled as to what had brought her there ; but
Mr. Ripley would never have got together the
prosperous business he had done had he not
also been a capital judge of human nature.
To ensure her being treated with much consideration, Sturton had thought proper to
confide to him a hint of Miss Eyre's previous
position. Mr. Ripley really did want a nice-
looking, lady-like woman for the purpose he
specified. Miss Eyre, he saw at a glance—
young though she was—was the very person
he was looking for. Two questions shot
through Ripley's mind. She was a lady by
birth, would she not be above her work?
Secondly, had she patience? And the fortnight's discipline he had prescribed, he

thought would be a pretty fair test of these
points.

Miss Eyre was very pleased with her newly
attained position. She was fairly popular with
her pupils, and was delighted to find that she
could earn quite sufficient money to keep Rory,
and proud at being further able to contribute
towards the household expenses. The two
slight drawbacks to her present situation were,
that Mr. Ripley never could refrain from
attempting to buy Rory, and also that she
was perpetually being asked to ride other horses
in the Park instead of her own. Like all
persons who have dealings with the noble
quadruped, her employer felt instinctively
that it behoved him to get a pull of some
shape in their mutual contract. Miss Eyre
was a fine horsewoman and gifted with
beautiful hands not only naturally but with
reference to dealing with a horse's mouth.
Mr. Ripley knew that a great many of his
hacks would be much improved by Miss

Eyre's handling, and could not resist the temptation of getting a bit of horse-breaking thrown in gratis ; the result was that Katie felt she had very little use for Rory, and though still resolute as ever not to part with him, yet grudged the expense of keeping him to do nothing. If she was to ride Ripley's horses, and it seemed now that there was always something that they wished Miss Eyre "just to give a canter to," she might as well send Rory to her sister. Mrs. Belton had told her, as soon as she heard that the horse had been brought to London, that she would always take charge of him if wanted. Aldershot was close by, and as colonel of a cavalry regiment Belton had plenty of stable room at his disposal. Accordingly Katie took advantage of her sister's offer and sent Rory down to Aldershot.

❋   ❋   ❋   ❋

Excitement is running high in our great military station, for time has slipped away since the Eyres left Rathkelly and settled at Hampstead. Winter is or should be past and gone, and we are on the verge of the race for the soldiers' blue ribbon. This year it is to be decided on the slopes of Esher. That Aldershot should be pretty full of talk and conversation concerning it, was but natural; at least half-a-dozen of the candidates were the property of men quartered there and were being trained in the vicinity.

Sturton has got leave from Plymouth, and is staying for a week with his regiment, and no one was more keenly interested. Sturton is a man who likes to win at whatever the game he may be playing, and though he undoubtedly can bear defeat without a sign of vexation, yet he would prefer looking on, to standing a forlorn chance. He had promised to ride for Belton and was assured that his mount was a good horse, but he was curious to judge for himself on this point.

"What's the regiment doing?" asked

Sturton, of one of his old cronies. "Is anyone running anything. Have any of you
got one fit to go?"

"We've only one to do battle for us, that
horse of Chester's that he rode at Callowtown."

"Of course, Loadstone! Well what does
he say about him?" enquired Sturton.

"I don't know," rejoined the other. "It's
a rum thing, but Tom is a changed man. He
has turned mysterious and won't talk. I don't
know what has come to him. He has never
been the same since we left Ireland. Perhaps
the whiskey this side of the Channel don't suit
him."

"Do you know who is to ride Loadstone?"

"Yes; and that's all I know about him.
Tom rides himself, but whether the horse is
doing well, and whether Tom fancies his
chance or not, he has confided to nobody."

That his old subaltern was somewhat
changed, Sturton discovered before he had

talked with him ten minutes, but nothing to
the extent that he had been represented. He
certainly was rather graver—graver and
more silent than he was wont to be—but that
Sturton could account for; he knew that
Chester had been very much in earnest in
his love for Katie Eyre ; and that his want of
success in that affair had been a severe blow to
him. " However," he had reflected, " he'll get
over it in course of time. I only hope, poor
beggar, it won't take him so long as it has
done me."

Sturton was putting up in a vacant quarter
next to Chester's, and before turning in, he
strolled into the latter's room for a final talk
and cigar.

" So, you're going to have a shy at the big
chase, Tom. Do you fancy your chance ? "

" Yes " ; replied the other, " very much !
Loadstone is wonderfully well, and I've tried
him a good bit better than I thought him ; I
mean to back him to win a good stake, and it

will be the fault of the man, not the horse, if it doesn't come off."

"Never fear, Tom; you're not likely to forget the lesson of last year; don't be in too great a hurry to get home," and then the conversation drifted into different channels—but one thing puzzled both men, when they separated. The name of Katie Eyre had never been mentioned between them. Chester never for a moment supposed that Sturton could have heard anything about the Eyres down at Plymouth; while Sturton, on his part, thought that Katie might not care to have her present employment talked about. Although neither of the men knew it, that young lady was domiciled within about a couple of miles of the camp at that minute. Katie had stuck most resolutely to her work for the last few months; and, though Mrs. Belton had given her many an invitation to run down to Aldershot, she had steadily refused them all. But she had heard much of the glories

of Sandown, and she had never seen a Grand
Military. Her brother-in-law had a horse
running in this one, and, what was more,
Captain Sturton was going to ride. She was
entitled to a short holiday, she would claim
it now. Another thing, why shouldn't her
father go too. It would be a nice outing for
him ; and as Katie said with a laugh, "No
man ever enjoyed a bit of divarsion more."
So she wrote to Grace, and speedily received
a reply to the effect that Mrs. Belton would
be only too delighted to put them both up for
the week. A brief absence from her duties
was easily arranged with Mr. Ripley, and the
same evening that saw Sturton's appearance
at the mess of his old regiment Mr. and Miss
Eyre sat down at the Belton's dinner table.

Sturton had found a note waiting for
him on his arrival at Aldershot from Mrs.
Belton, asking him to dine with them
the next day, and, accordingly, he stepped
into a fly next evening to fulfil that engage-

ment. He was a little surprised that Chester was not also asked; but, finally supposed that Belton wanted to have a long talk with him about the forthcoming race, and then dismissed the subject from his mind. Belton, no doubt, did not wish Chester to be present at their conversation. He was in good time, and when he entered the drawing-room, Harold Sturton was for once taken fairly aback. A young lady came forward to greet him that carried his memory back to a Callowtown ball of many years ago. He knew perfectly well that the young lady he was shaking hands with was Katie Eyre, but he could not help murmuring to himself, " how like," as he did so. To have taken one sister for the other would have been impossible, but the resemblance between Katie and Mrs. Belton had increased very much of late, and those who remembered Grace at her first ball would certainly have pronounced Katie very like what she was then. To people who saw

her constantly this growing likeness to
Grace was imperceptible, but Sturton, it must
be borne in mind, had not seen Miss Eyre for
close upon a twelvemonth, and this year
had transformed the school-girl into a woman.
He sat down beside her, and asked her how
she liked her new vocation?

"Very much," replied Katie. "I never
expected to make so much money nor find
work come so easy. Mr. Ripley is very kind
and considerate, and except that he covets
my horse dreadfully I've nothing to say
against him. No, except a stupid pupil now
and again, I've really nothing to grumble
at."

Here the entrance of Mrs. Belton, followed
by her father, interrupted their conversation.

"I've no one to meet you, Captain Sturton.
We're quite a family party. We have none
of us seen you for ever so long, especially my
father and Katie, and then, you know, we all
want to talk horse, and that might bore

people not so interested as we are in the race of to-morrow."

" Yes," laughed Belton, who had just made his appearance. " Horse is the prevailing topic in Aldershot at present. How are you, Sturton ? ' fit,' I hope ? Now, if you will take Katie, we'll go to dinner."

They were a very cheery party, as, indeed, they were bound to be. The Colonel was a man who gloried in garrison races, and had been a very fair performer until he got rather too heavy to ride. He was very sanguine about carrying off the Gold Cup, and in high spirits in consequence. Katie was thoroughly enjoying her well-earned holiday, while Mr. Eyre seemed to have thrown the " hard times " behind him, and looked ten years younger than in those latter days at Rath-kelly.

" Well, Sturton," he exclaimed, " you won for the family last year ; you'll have to do the same for us to-morrow. Here, George, we must all drink this toast; here's success to the Nabob."

The toast was laughingly drunk and then Colonel Belton replied gaily :

"Well, to return thanks now would be a little premature, but the horse is really as fit as he can be made, and I do think has a tremendous chance. We've tried him to be ten pounds better than Rory — that's good enough, isn't it."

"There must have been something wrong about the trial," exclaimed Miss Eyre. "I'm sure you haven't got a horse ten pounds better than Rory.'

"Perhaps not," replied the Colonel. "However, that's what we make it. That'll do Sturton, won't it?"

"I'm afraid not. Your pet is a good little horse, Miss Eyre, but the Nabob will have to meet one to-morrow that is quite that much better than Rory."

"What's that?" enquired Mrs. Belton.

"One that you saw behind him at Callow-town, that, I fancy, you'll never see behind him again—Loadstone."

"What, that horse of Chester's?" said Mr. Eyre. "By Jove, Sturton, you're right. If he hadn't made a mistake at that last bank, Loadstone would have won easily."

"Yes," replied Sturton. "He could have come away from me any time in the race. Tom tells me he has had a thoroughly satisfactory preparation at Melwood's. You'll see, he won't fall this time. I always back my own mount, but I mean to save on Loadstone, and should recommend everyone else to do the same."

"What do you think of Katie?" asked Mrs. Belton of Sturton, when, their cigarettes finished, the gentlemen had joined the ladies in the drawing-room. "Don't you see a great change in her?"

"Very great. She has, so to speak, grown up all of a sudden; how pluckily she has

faced her troubles, and how very like she
has grown to yourself."

"Ah! you see it, so they tell me with the
advantage of being a dozen years my junior.
It's a quare thing as they say in the old
country, but I declare poverty seems to have
agreed with Papa and Katie. Papa has not
been in such spirits for years, they tell me,
as he is now that he has very little money to
live upon. While, as for Katie, it has knocked
all the nonsense out of her. All the old
petulance has gone, and, thanks to you, she
is working bravely for her living, and enjoys
doing it." And here Mrs. Belton moved away
to speak to her father, and Sturton soon found
himself laughing and talking with Miss Eyre,
who amused him immensely by her account
of the doings of the riding school, and
Ripley's numerous and subtle endeavours to
buy Rory.

As Katie undressed that evening, she
thought with a smile of that little dinner at

Rathkelly about a year ago, at which she had been so intensely dissatisfied. A triumphant little smile played about her lips as she took a last peep in⁻ the glass and murmured, "Well, I can't complain that he took no notice of me this time!"

As for Harold Sturton, as he drove back to camp, he was plunged into intense thought.

"Deuced odd," he said to himself. "My life, like history, seems about to repeat itself."

CHAPTER XVI.

"THE SOLDIERS' BLUE RIBBON."

A FINE bright day towards the end of March, a day for furs and ulsters, a day on which, though the wind was, as might have been expected, in the East, it had moderated its vagaries, while the bright sun had an exhilarating effect upon the gay throng mustered on the lawn at Sandown. A great gathering this for the soldiers. Men from all parts of the kingdom have flocked to Esher on the chance of meeting old comrades, and to see the Gold Cup run for. Pretty well all the gentlemen riders in the country are gathered there, and the army has always contributed a large contingent to swell the

ranks of these last. Luncheons! There are
luncheons all over the course, from the Club
Rooms at the back of the stand to the
innumerable drags the other side of the
course. Whatever its shortcomings may be
upon service, the soldiers take care there
shall be no shortcomings in the commissariat
department when they go racing. There is a
goodly gathering of pretty women from
town, and a strong muster from the surrounding country, all looking their best and
their brightest. It was just the sort of day
which gave ladies both a colour and an
appetite, and this latter their male belongings
stand in much need of on the day of the
Grand Military, when everyone is expected
to lunch at least three or four times.
The Eyres and Beltons had arrived at
Sandown in good time, and the Colonel's
carriage had taken up an excellent position
on the far side of the course. Sturton
speedily joined them there, and the Colonel

at once exclaimed, " Have you seen the
Nabob? "

" Yes," he replied, " I've just come from
the paddock. Your groom has done him
every justice, but you've no pull over Loadstone in that respect. He looks fine as a
star and trained to an hour. They are back-
ing him in there," and Sturton nodded his
head in the direction of the ring, " for pounds,
shillings, and pence, and only that Chester is
an unknown man between the flags, the
partisans of Melwood's stable would have to
be content with a short price. How do you
do, Miss Eyre. I only hope I shall be as
lucky to-day as I was at Callowtown."

" I've every confidence in you," said
Mrs. Belton. " Don't forget you're to dine
with us again to celebrate, I hope, your
victory."

" Yes, ' the Cup ' must be christened," remarked Katie.

" A rather premature counting of chickens,

eh, Sturton?" cried Mr. Eyre. "It would
be odd if Chester turned the tables on you."

"Nothing more probable, and if I can't
win I hope he may. Please Tom awfully.
He's dangerous to-day. Not cock-a-hoop,
but quietly confident. Now I'm off. You
know my superstition about *first out.*"

"First in," said Mrs. Belton. "*Au
revoir.*"

Sturton made his way rapidly to where the
Nabob was walking about, and was quickly
in the saddle. True to his old whim, he was
about to head the procession out of the
paddock, when Belton suddenly called to him.
Sturton checked his horse only to hear that
the Colonel had backed Loadstone also for
a little. But during this slight pause Chester
passed him, and when they filed out on to
the course Loadstone was leading.

"That looks ominous," exclaims Mrs. Belton,
as the horses walked past the stand.

"Very," said Katie, in a low voice.

The girl was quite as anxious that the Nabob should win as her sister, but from a different motive. Mrs. Belton wished the horse to win, Katie was only desirous of the man's success.

Although Sturton had this whim, and was just a little annoyed with Belton for having caused him to miss gratifying it, he was the last man to be cast down because the augury was unfavourable. It was somewhat on the principle of the old whist-player's remark on winning the cut and choice of seats: "I don't believe myself in the luck of the hinges, but we may as well have 'em for all that."

The preliminary canter is soon over, and as they go by, the followers of Melwood's stable are well pleased with the long, slashing stride of their pet. "If he can but ride him, if he can only hold him," they murmur, "he'll win easy enough, never fear."

Loadstone, as Sturton knew, had always been a hot horse, but Chester had given his old mentor no hint of the tactics he meant to pursue. As they walked down to the post Sturton commented on the large sums of money for which Loadstone had been backed.

"Yes," replied Chester. "I'm standing him for a good stake myself, but I told them in the stable from the very first that I intended to ride him, so that if I muff it, they have no business to blame me if it's a case of spilt milk."

Arrived at the post the lot were speedily despatched on their journey, and no sooner had they settled down than Loadstone was seen at the head of affairs, and there he remained till somewhere about a mile had been covered, when he was pulled back. Sturton, who had made up his mind that this was the most dangerous horse in the race, at first hoped that Loadstone had somewhat over-powered his rider, but he soon saw that Chester deemed it more judicious to give his horse his head than to fight with him, but that for all that he had not at all lost control over him. A mile from home Sturton, who had been lying off, begins to creep to the front, the Nabob is going well and jumping faultlessly, but as his rider comes alongside Loadstone, he sees that he is full of running and still pulling hard at his bridle.

" I'm done," remarks the captain to himself. " If his horse doesn't make a mistake, Chester can't lose, and though Loadstone is pulling he is jumping in most temperate fashion." By the time they near the last fence there are only three left in it, and Chester is palpably in racing parlance, " lying over " his two opponents.

" It was the last fence did him before," muttered Sturton. " I'll not throw up the sponge till I've seen him over that."

But Chester had not forgotten the lesson at Callowtown. He pulled his horse well together at the last jump, and, safely over, just shook him up and sailed in an easy

winner by seven or eight lengths. A good
race for second money ending in the defeat
of the Nabob by a neck.

"Oh dear, oh dear!" exclaimed Mrs.
Belton, "this is a terrible blow. What shall
we do, Katie? And to think we have asked
Captain Sturton to dinner too."

"It is very sad," said Miss Eyre, with mock
gravity. "It amounts to a domestic bereave-
ment. Last night we quite reckoned that
Gold Cup as one of the family."

"Oh, well!" laughed her father. "I daresay we shall bear up against it. I think one
has pleasanter times with empty pockets than
with full ones," with which cheery, but very
Hibernian remark, and an exclamation that
he was dying with hunger, Mr. Eyre plunged
into a plethoric looking hamper.

Mr. Eyre proved a true prophet. It would
have been difficult for five people to be
merrier than were Mrs. Belton and her
guests that evening, and as the sisters went

upstairs that night after Sturton's departure, the former said, "you've had the best of me a good deal to-day, Katie. I've lost the Gold Cup and you, my dear, have won something a good deal better worth keeping."

"Oh, Grace," rejoined the girl, as she ran off to her own room.

Terence Flynn soon found employment in the vicinity of Hampstead, and was very shortly in a position to offer Norah a home, but neither of them have any disposition to return to the "ould counthry."

THE END.

PRINTED BY
KELLY AND CO., GATE STREET, LINCOLN'S INN FIELDS, W.C.,
AND KINGSTON-ON-THAMES.

www.ingramcontent.com/pod-product-compliance
Lightning Source LLC
Chambersburg PA
CBHW020347030726
47496CB00007B/2038